THE TWO-GUN MAN

Copyright © 2007 BiblioBazaar
All rights reserved
ISBN: 978-1-4264-9919-7

Original copyright: 1911

CHARLES ALDEN SELTZER
Author of "The Range Riders," "The Coming of the Law," etc.

THE TWO-GUN MAN

THE TWO-GUN MAN

CONTENTS

CHAPTER
- I THE STRANGER AT DRY BOTTOM 9
- II THE STRANGER SHOOTS 14
- III THE CABIN IN THE FLAT 19
- IV A "DIFFERENT GIRL" 28
- V THE MAN OF DRY BOTTOM 39
- VI AT THE TWO DIAMOND 43
- VII HE MEASURE OF A MAN 48
- VIII THE FINDING OF THE ORPHAN 59
- IX WOULD YOU BE A "CHARACTER"? 64
- X DISAPPEARANCE OF THE ORPHAN 70
- XI A TOUCH OF LOCAL COLOR 76
- XII THE STORY BEGINS 83
- XIII "DO YOU SMOKE?" 92
- XIV ON THE EDGE OF THE PLATEAU 98
- XV A FREE HAND 113
- XVI LEVIATT TAKES A STEP 118
- XVII BREAK IN THE STORY 131
- XVIII THE DIM TRAIL 141
- XIX THE SHOT IN THE DARK 148
- XX LOVE AND A RIFLE 153
- XXI THE PROMISE 159
- XXII KEEPING A PROMISE 163
- XXIII AT THE EDGE OF THE COTTONWOOD 176
- XXIV THE END OF THE STORY 183

CHAPTER I

THE STRANGER AT DRY BOTTOM

From the crest of Three Mile Slope the man on the pony could see the town of Dry Bottom straggling across the gray floor of the flat, its low, squat buildings looking like so many old boxes blown there by an idle wind, or unceremoniously dumped there by a careless fate and left, regardless, to carry out the scheme of desolation.

Apparently the rider was in no hurry, for, as the pony topped the rise and the town burst suddenly into view, the little animal pricked up its ears and quickened its pace, only to feel the reins suddenly tighten and to hear the rider's voice gruffly discouraging haste. Therefore, the pony pranced gingerly, alert, champing the bit impatiently, picking its way over the lumpy hills of stone and cactus, but holding closely to the trail.

The man lounged in the saddle, his strong, well-knit body swaying gracefully, his eyes, shaded by the brim of his hat, narrowed with slight mockery and interest as he gazed steadily at the town that lay before him.

"I reckon that must be Dry Bottom," he said finally, mentally taking in its dimensions. "If that's so, I've only got twenty miles to go."

Half way down the slope, and still a mile and a half from the town, the rider drew the pony to a halt. He dropped the reins over the high pommel of the saddle, drew out his two guns, one after the other, rolled the cylinders, and returned the guns to their holsters. He had heard something of Dry Bottom's reputation and in examining his pistols he was merely preparing himself for an emergency. For a moment after he had replaced the weapons he sat quietly in the saddle. Then he shook out the reins, spoke to the pony, and the little animal set forward at a slow lope.

An ironic traveler, passing through Dry Bottom in its younger days, before civic spirit had definitely centered its efforts upon things nomenclatural, had hinted that the town should be known as "dry" because of the fact that while it boasted seven buildings, four were saloons; and that "bottom" might well be used as a suffix, because, in the nature of things, a town of seven buildings, four of which were saloons, might reasonably expect to descend to the very depths of moral iniquity.

The ironic traveler had spoken with prophetic wisdom. Dry Bottom was trying as best it knew how to wallow in the depths of sin. Unlovely, soiled, desolate of verdure, dumped down upon a flat of sand in a treeless waste, amid cactus, crabbed yucca, scorpions, horned toads, and rattlesnakes. Dry Bottom had forgotten its morals, subverted its principles, and neglected its God.

As the rider approached to within a few hundred yards of the edge of town he became aware of a sudden commotion. He reined in his pony, allowing it to advance at a walk, while with alert eyes he endeavored to search out the cause of the excitement. He did not have long to watch for the explanation.

A man had stepped out of the door of one of the saloons, slowly walking twenty feet away from it toward the center of the street. Immediately other men had followed. But these came only to a point just outside the door. For some reason which was not apparent to the rider, they were giving the first man plenty of room.

The rider was now able to distinguish the faces of the men in the group, and he gazed with interested eyes at the man who had first issued from the door of the saloon.

The man was tall—nearly as tall as the rider—and in his every movement seemed sure of himself. He was young, seemingly about thirty-five, with shifty, insolent eyes and a hard mouth whose lips were just now curved into a self-conscious smile.

The rider had now approached to within fifty feet of the man, halting his pony at the extreme end of the hitching rail that skirted the front of the saloon. He sat carelessly in the saddle, his gaze fixed on the man.

The men who had followed the first man out, to the number of a dozen, were apparently deeply interested, though plainly skeptical. A short, fat man, who was standing near the saloon door, looked on with a half-sneer. Several others were smiling blandly. A tall man on the extreme edge of the crowd, near the rider, was watching the man in the street gravely. Other men had allowed various expressions to creep into their faces. But all were silent.

Not so the man in the street. Plainly, here was conceit personified, and yet a conceit mingled with a maddening insolence. His expression told all that this thing which he was about to do was worthy of the closest attention. He was the axis upon which the interest of the universe revolved.

Certainly he knew of the attention he was attracting. Men were approaching from the other end of the street, joining the group in front of the saloon—which the rider now noticed was called the "Silver Dollar." The newcomers were inquisitive; they spoke in low tones to the men who had arrived before them, gravely inquiring the cause.

But the man in the street seemed not disturbed by his rapidly swelling audience. He stood in the place he had selected, his insolent eyes roving over the assembled company, his thin, expressive lips opening a very little to allow words to filter through them.

"Gents," he said, "you're goin' to see some shootin'! I told you in the Silver Dollar that I could keep a can in the air while I put five holes in it. There's some of you gassed about bein' showed, not believin'. An' now I'm goin' to show you!"

He reached down and took up a can that had lain at his feet, removing the red lithographed label, which had a picture of a large tomato in the center of it. The can was revealed, naked and shining in the white sunlight. The man placed the can in his left hand and drew his pistol with the right.

Then he tossed the can into the air. While it still rose his weapon exploded, the can shook spasmodically and turned clear over. Then in rapid succession followed four other explosions, the last occurring just before the can reached the ground. The man smiled, still holding the smoking weapon in his hand.

The tall man on the extreme edge of the group now stepped forward and examined the can, while several other men crowded about to look. There were exclamations of surprise. It was curious to see how quickly enthusiasm and awe succeeded skepticism.

"He's done it, boys!" cried the tall man, holding the can aloft. "Bored it in five places!" He stood erect, facing the crowd. "I reckon that's some shootin'!" He now threw a glance of challenge and defiance about him. "I've got a hundred dollars to say that there ain't another man in this here town can do it!"

Several men tried, but none equaled the first man's performance. Many of the men could not hit the can at all. The first man watched their efforts, sneers twitching his lips as man after man failed.

Presently all had tried. Watching closely, the rider caught an expression of slight disappointment on the tall man's face. The rider was the only man who had not yet tried his skill with the pistol, and the man in the street now looked up at him, his eyes glittering with an insolent challenge. As it happened, the rider glanced at the shooter at the instant the latter had turned to look up at him. Their eyes met fairly, the shooter's conveying a silent taunt. The rider smiled, slight mockery glinting his eyes.

Apparently the stranger did not care to try his skill. He still sat lazily in the saddle, his gaze wandering languidly over the crowd. The latter plainly expected him to take part in the shooting match and was impatient over his inaction.

"Two-gun," sneered a man who stood near the saloon door. "I wonder what he totes them two guns for?"

The shooter heard and turned toward the man who had spoken, his lips wreathed satirically.

"I reckon he wouldn't shoot nothin' with them," he said, addressing the man who had spoken.

Several men laughed. The tall man who had revealed interest before now raised a hand, checking further comment.

"That offer of a hundred to the man who can beat that shootin' still goes," he declared. "An' I'm taking off the condition. The man that tries don't have to belong to Dry Bottom. No stranger is barred!"

The stranger's glance again met the shooter's. The latter grinned felinely. Then the rider spoke. The crowd gave him its polite attention.

"I reckon you-all think you've seen some shootin'," he said in a steady, even voice, singularly free from boast. "But I reckon you ain't seen any real shootin'." He turned to the tall, grave-faced man. "I ain't got no hundred," he said, "but I'm goin' to show you."

He still sat in the saddle. But now with an easy motion he swung down and hitched his pony to the rail.

CHAPTER II

THE STRANGER SHOOTS

The stranger seemed taller on the ground than in the saddle and an admirable breadth of shoulder and slenderness of waist told eloquently of strength. He could not have been over twenty-five or six. Yet certain hard lines about his mouth, the glint of mockery in his eyes, the pronounced forward thrust of the chin, the indefinable force that seemed to radiate from him, told the casual observer that here was a man who must be approached with care.

But apparently the shooter saw no such signs. In the first glance that had been exchanged between the two men there had been a lack of ordinary cordiality. And now, as the rider slid down from his pony and advanced toward the center of the street, the shooter's lips curled. Writhing through them came slow-spoken words.

"You runnin' sheep, stranger?"

The rider's lips smiled, but his eyes were steady and cold. In them shone a flash of cold humor. He stood, quietly contemplating his insulter.

Smiles appeared on the faces of several of the onlookers. The tall man with the grave face watched with a critical eye. The insult had been deliberate, and many men crouched, plainly expecting a serious outcome. But the stranger made no move toward his guns, and when he answered he might have been talking about the weather, so casual was his tone.

"I reckon you think you're a plum man," he said quietly. "But if you are, you ain't showed it much—buttin' in with that there wise observation.

An' there's some men who think that shootin' at a man is more excitin' than shootin' at a can."

There was a grim quality in his voice now. He leaned forward slightly, his eyes cold and alert. The shooter sneered experimentally. Again the audience smiled.

But the tall man now stepped forward. "You've made your play, stranger," he said quietly. "I reckon it's up to you to make good."

"Correct," agreed the stranger. "I'm goin' to show you some real shootin'. You got another can?"

Some one dived into the Silver Dollar and returned in a flash with another tomato can. This the stranger took, removing the label, as the shooter had done. Then, smiling, he took a position in the center of the street, the can in his right hand.

He did not draw his weapon as the shooter had done, but stood loosely in his place, his right hand still grasping the can, the left swinging idly by his side. Apparently he did not mean to shoot. Sneers reached the faces of several men in the crowd. The shooter growled, "Fourflush."

There was a flash as the can rose twenty feet in the air, propelled by the right hand of the stranger. As the can reached the apex of its climb the stranger's right hand descended and grasped the butt of the weapon at his right hip. There was a flash as the gun came out; a gasp of astonishment from the watchers. The can was arrested in the first foot of its descent by the shock of the first bullet striking it. It jumped up and out and again began its interrupted fall, only to stop dead still in the air as another bullet struck it. There was an infinitesimal pause, and then twice more the can shivered and jumped. No man in the crowd but could tell that the bullets were striking true.

The can was still ten feet in the air and well out from the stranger. The latter whipped his weapon to a level, the bullet striking the can and driving it twenty feet from him. Then it dropped. But when it was within five feet of the ground the stranger's gun spoke again. The can leaped, careened sideways, and fell, shattered, to the street, thirty feet distant from the stranger.

Several men sprang forward to examine it.

"Six times!" ejaculated the tall man in an awed tone. "An' he didn't pull his gun till he'd throwed the can!"

He approached the stranger, drawing him confidentially aside. The crowd slowly dispersed, loudly proclaiming the stranger's ability with the six-shooter. The latter took his honors lightly, the mocking smile again on his face.

"I'm lookin' for a man who can shoot," said the tall man, when the last man of the crowd had disappeared into the saloon.

The stranger smiled. "I reckon you've just seen some shootin'," he returned.

The tall man smiled mirthlessly. "You particular about what you shoot at?" he inquired.

The stranger's lips straightened coldly. "I used to have that habit," he returned evenly.

"Hard luck?" queried the tall man.

"I'm rollin' in wealth," stated the stranger, with an ironic sneer.

The tall man's eyes glittered. "Where you from?" he questioned.

"You c'n have three guesses," returned the stranger, his eyes narrowing with the mockery that the tall man had seen in them before.

The tall man adopted a placative tone. "I ain't wantin' to butt into your business," he said. "I was wantin' to find out if any one around here knowed you."

"This town didn't send any reception committee to meet me, did they?" smiled the stranger.

"Correct," said the tall man. He leaned closer. "You willin' to work your guns for me for a hundred a month?"

The stranger looked steadily into the tall man's eyes.

"You've been right handy askin' questions," he said. "Mebbe you'll answer some. What's your name?"

"Stafford," returned the tall man. "I'm managin' the Two Diamond, over on the Ute."

The stranger's eyelashes flickered slightly. His eyes narrowed quizzically. "What you wantin' of a gun-man?" he asked.

"Rustler," returned the other shortly.

The stranger smiled. "Figger on shootin' him?" he questioned.

Stafford hesitated. "Well, no," he returned. "That is, not until I'm sure I've got the right one." He seized the stranger's arm in a confidential grip. "You see," he explained, "I don't know just where I'm at. There's been a rustler workin' on the herd, an' I ain't been able to get close enough to find out who it is. But rustlin' has got to be stopped. I've sent over to Raton to get a man named Ned Ferguson, who's been workin' for Sid Tucker, of the Lazy J. Tucker wrote me quite a while back, tellin' me that this man was plum slick at nosin' out rustlers. He was to come to the Two Diamond two weeks ago. But he ain't showed up, an' I've about concluded that he ain't comin'. An' so I come over to Dry Bottom to find a man."

"You've found one," smiled the stranger.

Stafford drew out a handful of double eagles and pressed them into the other's hand. "I'm goin' over to the Two Diamond now," he said. "You'd better wait a day or two, so's no one will get wise. Come right to me, like you was wantin' a job."

He started toward the hitching rail for his pony, hesitated and then walked back.

"I didn't get your name," he smiled.

The stranger's eyes glittered humorously. "It's Ferguson," he said quietly.

Stafford's eyes widened with astonishment. Then his right hand went out and grasped the other's.

"Well, now," he said warmly, "that's what I call luck."

Ferguson smiled. "Mebbe it's luck," he returned. "But before I go over to work for you there's got to be an understandin'. I c'n shoot some," he continued, looking steadily at Stafford, "but I ain't runnin' around the country shootin' men without cause. I'm willin' to try an' find your rustler for you, but I ain't shootin' him—unless he goes to crowdin' me mighty close."

"I'm agreein' to that," returned Stafford.

He turned again, looking back over his shoulder. "You'll sure be over?" he questioned.

"I'll be there the day after to-morrow," stated Ferguson.

He turned and went into the Silver Dollar. Stafford mounted his pony and loped rapidly out of town.

CHAPTER III

THE CABIN IN THE FLAT

It was the day appointed by Ferguson for his presence at the Two Diamond ranch, and he was going to keep his word. Three hours out of Dry Bottom he had struck the Ute trail and was loping his pony through a cottonwood that skirted the river. It was an enchanted country through which he rode; a land of vast distances, of white sunlight, blue skies, and clear, pure air. Mountains rose in the distances, their snowcapped peaks showing above the clouds like bald rock spires above the calm level of the sea. Over the mountains swam the sun, its lower rim slowly disappearing behind the peaks, throwing off broad white shafts of light that soon began to dim as vari-colors, rising in a slumberous haze like a gauze veil, mingled with them.

Ferguson's gaze wandered from the trail to the red buttes that fringed the river. He knew this world; there was no novelty here for him. He knew the lava beds, looming gray and dead beneath the foothills; he knew the grotesque rock shapes that seemed to hint of a mysterious past. Nature had not altered her face. On the broad levels were the yellow tinted lines that told of the presence of soap-weed, the dark lines that betrayed the mesquite, the saccatone belts that marked the little guillies. Then there were the barrancas, the arid stretches where the sage-brush and the cactus grew. Snaky octilla dotted the space; the crabbed yucca had not lost its ugliness.

Ferguson looked upon the world with unseeing eyes. He had lived here long and the country had not changed. It would never change. Nothing ever changed here but the people.

But he himself had not changed. Twenty-seven years in this country was a long time, for here life was not measured by age, but by experience. Looking back over the years he could see that he was living to-day as he had lived last year, as he had lived during the last decade—a hard life, but having its compensations.

His coming to the Two Diamond ranch was merely another of those incidents that, during the past year, had broken the monotony of range life for him. He had had some success in breaking up a band of cattle thieves which had made existence miserable for Sid Tucker, his employer, and the latter had recommended him to Stafford. The promise of high wages had been attractive, and so he had come. He had not expected to surprise any one. When during his conversation with the tall man in Dry Bottom he had discovered that the latter was the man for whom he was to work he had been surprised himself. But he had not revealed his surprise. Experience and association with men who kept their emotions pretty much to themselves had taught him the value of repression when in the presence of others.

But alone he allowed his emotions full play. There was no one to see, no one to hear, and the silence and the distances, and the great, swimming blue sky would not tell.

Stafford's action in coming to Dry Bottom for a gunfighter had puzzled him not a little. Apparently the Two Diamond manager was intent upon the death of the rustler he had mentioned. He had been searching for a man who could "shoot," he had said. Ferguson had interpreted this to mean that he desired to employ a gunfighter who would not scruple to kill any man he pointed out, whether innocent or guilty. He had had some experience with unscrupulous ranch managers, and he had admired them very little. Therefore, during the ride today, his lips had curled sarcastically many times.

Riding through a wide clearing in the cottonwood, he spoke a thought that had troubled him not a little since he had entered Stafford's employ.

"Why," he said, as he rode along, sitting carelessly in the saddle, "he's wantin' to make a gunfighter out of me. But I reckon I ain't goin' to shoot no man unless I'm pretty sure he's gunnin' for me." His lips curled ironically. "I wonder what the boys of the Lazy J would think if they knew that a guy was tryin' to make a gunfighter out of their old straw boss. I reckon they'd think that guy was loco—or a heap mistaken in his man. But I'm seein' this thing through. I ain't ridin' a hundred miles just to take a look at the man who's hirin' me. It'll be a change. An' when I go back to the Lazy J—"

It was not the pony's fault. Neither was it Ferguson's. The pony was experienced; behind his slant eyes was stored a world of horse-wisdom that had pulled him and his rider through many tight places. And Ferguson had ridden horses all his life; he would not have known what to do without one.

But the pony stumbled. The cause was a prairie-dog hole, concealed under a clump of matted mesquite. Ferguson lunged forward, caught at the saddle horn, missed it, and pitched head-foremost out of the saddle, turning completely over and alighting upon his feet. He stood erect for an instant, but the momentum had been too great. He went down, and when he tried to rise a twinge of pain in his right ankle brought a grimace to his face. He arose and hopped over to a flat rock, near where his pony now stood grazing as though nothing had happened.

Drawing off his boot, Ferguson made a rapid examination of the ankle. It was inflamed and painful, but not broken. He believed he could see it swelling. He rubbed it, hoping to assuage the pain. The woolen sock interfered with the rubbing, and he drew it off.

For a few minutes he worked with the ankle, but to little purpose. He finally became convinced that it was a bad sprain, and he looked up, scowling. The pony turned an inquiring eye upon him, and he grinned, suddenly smitten with the humor of the situation.

"You ain't got no call to look so doggoned innocent about it," he said. "If you'd been tendin' to your business, you wouldn't have stepped into no damned gopher hole."

The pony moved slowly away, and he looked whimsically after it, remarking: "Mebbe if I'd been tendin' to my business it wouldn't have happened, either." He spoke again to the pony. "I reckon you know that too, Mustard. You're some wise."

The animal was now at some little distance from the rock upon which he was sitting. He arose, hobbling on one foot toward it, carrying the discarded boot in his hand. He thought of riding with the foot bare. At the Two Diamond he was sure to find some sort of liniment which, with the help of a bandage, would materially assist nature in—

He was passing a filmy mesquite clump—the bare foot swinging wide. There was a warning rattle; a sharp thrust of a flat, brown head.

Ferguson halted in astonishment, almost knocked off his balance with the suddenness of the attack. He still held the boot, his fingers gripping it tightly. He raised it, with a purely involuntary motion, as though to hurl it at his insidious enemy. But he did not. The arm fell to his side, and his face slowly whitened. He stared dully and uncomprehendingly at the sinuous shape that was slipping noiselessly away through the matted grass.

Somehow, he had never thought of being bitten by a rattler. He had seen so many of them that he had come to look upon them only as targets at which he might shoot when he thought he needed practice. And now he was bitten. The unreality of the incident surprised him. He looked around at the silent hills, at the sun that swam above the mountain peaks, at the great, vast arc of sky that yawned above him. Hills, sky, and sun seemed also unreal. It was as though he had been suddenly thrust into a land of dreams.

But presently the danger of the situation burst upon him, and he lived once more in the reality. He looked down at his foot. A livid, pin-point wound showed in the flesh beside the arch. A tiny stream of blood was oozing from it. He forgot the pain of the sprained ankle and stood upon both feet, his body suddenly rigid, his face red with a sudden, consuming anger, shaking a tense fist at the disappearing rattler.

"You damned sneak!" he shouted shrilly.

In the same instant he had drawn one of his heavy guns and swung it over his head. Its crashing report brought a sudden swishing from beneath the grass, and he hopped over closer and sent three more bullets into the threshing brown body. He stood over it for a moment, his teeth showing in a savage snarl.

"You won't bite any one else, damn you!" he shouted.

The impotence of this conduct struck him immediately. He flushed and drooped his head, a grim smile slowly wearing down his expression of panic. Seldom did he allow his emotions to reveal themselves so plainly. But the swiftness of the rattler's attack, the surprise when he had not been thinking of such a thing, the fact that he was far from help and that his life was in danger—all had a damaging effect upon his self-control. And yet the smile showed that he was still master of himself.

Very deliberately he returned to the rock upon which he had been sitting, ripping off his coat and tearing away the sleeve of his woollen shirt. Twisting the sleeve into the form of a rude rope, he tied it loosely around his leg, just above the ankle. Then he thrust his knife between the improvised rope and the leg, forming a crude tourniquet. He twisted the knife until tears of pain formed in his eyes. Then he fastened the knife by tucking the haft under the rope. His movements had been very deliberate, but sure, and in a few minutes he hobbled to his pony and swung into the saddle.

He had seen men who had been bitten by rattlers—had seen them die. And he knew that if he did not get help within half an hour there would be little use of doing anything further. In half an hour the virus would have so great a grip upon him that it would be practically useless to apply any of the antidotes commonly known to the inhabitants of the country.

Inquiries that he had made at Dry Bottom had resulted in the discovery that the Two Diamond ranch was nearly thirty miles from the town. If he had averaged eight miles an hour he had covered about twenty-four miles of the distance. That would still leave about six. And he could not hope to ride those six miles in time to get any benefit from an antidote.

His lips straightened, he stared grimly at a ridge of somber hills that fringed the skyline. They had told him back in Dry Bottom that the Two Diamond ranch was somewhere in a big basin below those hills.

"I reckon I won't get there, after all," he said, commenting aloud.

Thereafter he rode grimly on, keeping a good grip upon himself—for he had seen men bitten by rattlers who had lost their self-control—and they had not been good to look upon. Much depended upon coolness; somewhere he had heard that it was a mistake for a bitten man to exert himself in the first few minutes following a bite; exertion caused the virus to circulate more rapidly through the system. And so he rode at an even pace, carefully avoiding the rough spots, though keeping as closely to the trail as possible.

"If it hadn't been a diamond-back—an' a five-foot one—this rope that I've got around my leg might be enough to fool him," he said once, aloud. "But I reckon he's got me." His eyes lighted savagely for an instant. "But I got him, too. Had the nerve to think that he could get away after throwin' his hooks into me."

Presently his eyes caught the saffron light that glowed in the western sky. He laughed with a grim humor. "I've heard tell that a snake don't die till sundown—much as you hurt him. If that's so, an' I don't get to where I c'n get some help, I reckon it'll be a stand off between him an' me as to who's goin' first."

A little later he drew Mustard to a halt, sitting very erect in the saddle and fixing his gaze upon a tall cottonwood tree that rose near the trail.

His heart was racing madly, and in spite of his efforts, he felt himself swaying from side to side. He had often seen a rattler doing that—flat, ugly head raised above his coiled body, forked tongue shooting out, his venomous eyes glittering, the head and the part of the body rising above the coils swaying gracefully back and forth. Yes, gracefully, for in spite of his hideous aspect, there was a certain horrible ease of movement about a rattler—a slippery, sinuous motion that partly revealed reserve strength, and hinted at repressed energy.

Many times, while watching them, he had been fascinated by their grace, and now, sitting in the saddle, he caught himself wondering if the influence of a bite were great enough to cause the person bitten to imitate the snake. He laughed when this thought struck him and drove his spurs sharply against Mustard's flanks, riding forward past the cottonwood at which he had been staring.

"Hell!" he ejaculated, as he passed the tree, "what a fool notion."

But he could not banish the "notion" from his mind, and five minutes later, when he tried again to sit steadily, he found the swaying more pronounced. The saddle seemed to rock with him, and even by jamming his uninjured foot tightly into the ox-bow stirrup he could not stop swaying.

"Mebbe I won't get very far," he said, realizing that the poison had entered his system, and that presently it would riot in his veins, "but I'm goin' on until I stop. I wouldn't want that damned rattler to know that he'd made me quit so soon."

He urged Mustard to a faster pace, even while realizing that speed was hopeless. He could never reach the Two Diamond. Convinced of this, he halted the pony again, swaying in the saddle and holding, for the first time, to the pommel in an effort to steady himself. But he still swayed. He laughed mockingly.

"Now, what do you think of that?" he said, addressing the silence. "You might think I was plum tenderfoot an' didn't know how to ride a horse proper."

He urged the pony onward again, and for some little time rode with bowed head, trying to keep himself steady by watching the trail. He rode through a little clearing, where the grass was matted and some naked rocks reared aloft. Near a clump of sage-brush he saw a sudden movement—a rattler trying to slip away unnoticed. But the snake slid into Ferguson's vision and with a sneer of hate he drew one of his weapons and whipped it over his head, its roar awakening echoes in the wood. Twice, three times, the crashing report sounded. But the rattler whisked away and disappeared into the grass—apparently uninjured.

For an instant Ferguson scowled. Then a grin of mockery reached his flushed face.

"I reckon I'm done," he said. "Can't even hit a rattler no more, an' him a brother or sister of that other one." A delirious light flashed suddenly in his eyes, and he seemed on the point of dismounting. "I'll cert'nly smash you some!" he said, speaking to the snake—which he could no longer see. "I ain't goin' to let no snake bite me an' get away with it!"

But he now smiled guiltily, embarrassment shining in his eyes. "I reckon that wasn't the snake that bit you, Ferguson," he said. "The one that bit you is back on the trail. He ain't goin' to die till sundown. Not till sundown," he repeated mechanically, grimly; "Ferguson ain't goin' to die till sundown."

He rode on, giving no attention to the pony whatever, but letting the reins fall and holding to the pommel of the saddle. His face was burning now, his hands were twitching, and an unnatural gleam had come into his eyes.

"Ferguson got hooked by a rattler!" he suddenly exclaimed, hilarity in his voice. "He run plum into that reptile; tried to walk on him with a bare foot." The laugh was checked as suddenly as it had come, and a grim quality entered his voice. "But Ferguson wasn't no tenderfoot—he didn't scare none. He went right on, not sayin' anything. You see, he was reckonin' to be man's size."

He rode on a little way, and as he entered another clearing a rational gleam came into his eyes. "I'm still a-goin' it," he muttered.

A shadow darkened the trail; he heard Mustard whinny. He became aware of a cabin in front of him; heard an exclamation; saw dimly the slight figure of a woman, sitting on a small porch; as through a mist, he saw her rise and approach him, standing on the edge of the porch, looking at him.

He smiled, bowing low to her over his pony's mane.

"I shot him, ma'am," he said gravely, "but he ain't goin' to die till sundown."

As from some great distance a voice seemed to come to him. "Mercy!" it said. "What is wrong? Who is shot?"

"Why, the snake, ma'am," he returned thickly. He slid down from his pony and staggered to the edge of the porch, leaning against one of the slender posts and hanging dizzily on. "You see, ma'am, that damned rattler got Ferguson. But Ferguson ain't reckonin' on dyin' till sundown. He couldn't let no snake get the best of him."

He saw the woman start toward him, felt her hands on his arms, helping him upon the porch. Then he felt her hands on his shoulders, felt them pressing him down. He felt dimly that there was a chair under him, and he sank into it, leaning back and stretching himself out full length. A figure flitted before him and presently there was a sharp pain in his foot. He started out of the chair, and was abruptly shoved back into it, Then the figure leaned over him, prying his jaws apart with some metal like object and pouring something down his throat. He clicked as he swallowed, vainly trying to brush away the object.

"You're a hell of a snake," he said savagely. Then the world blurred dizzily, and he drifted into oblivion.

CHAPTER IV

A "DIFFERENT GIRL"

Ferguson had no means of knowing how long he was unconscious, but when he awoke the sun had gone down and the darkening shadows had stolen into the clearing near the cabin. He still sat in the chair on the porch. He tried to lift his injured foot and found to his surprise that some weight seemed to be on it. He struggled to an erect position, looking down. His foot had been bandaged, and the weight that he had thought was upon it was not a weight at all, but the hands of a young woman.

She sat on the porch floor, the injured foot in her lap, and she had just finished bandaging it. Beside her on the porch floor was a small black medicine case, a sponge, some yards of white cloth, and a tin wash basin partly filled with water.

He had a hazy recollection of the young woman; he knew it must have been she that he had seen when he had ridden up to the porch. He also had a slight remembrance of having spoken to her, but what the words were he could not recall. He stretched himself painfully. The foot pained frightfully, and his face felt hot and feverish; he was woefully weak and his nerves were tingling—but he was alive.

The girl looked up at his movement. Her lips opened and she held up a warning hand.

"You are to be very quiet," she admonished.

He smiled weakly and obeyed her, leaning back, his gaze on the slate-blue of the sky. She still worked at the foot, fastening the bandage; he could feel her fingers as they passed lightly over it. He did not move, feeling a deep contentment.

Presently she arose, placed the foot gently down, and entered the house. With closed eyes he lay in the chair, listening to her step as she walked about in the house. He lay there a long time, and when he opened his eyes again he knew that he must have been asleep, for the night had come and a big yellow moon was rising over a rim of distant hills. Turning his head slightly, he saw the interior of one of the rooms of the cabin—the kitchen, for he saw a stove and some kettles and pans hanging on the wall and near the window a table, over which was spread a cloth. A small kerosene lamp stood in the center of the table, its rays glimmering weakly through the window. He raised one hand and passed it over his forehead. There was still some fever, but he felt decidedly better than when he had awakened the first time.

Presently he heard a light step and became aware of some one standing near him. He knew it was the girl, even before she spoke, for he had caught the rustle of her dress.

"Are you awake," she questioned.

"Why, yes, ma'am," he returned. He turned to look at her, but in the darkness he could not see her face.

"Do you feel like eating anything?" she asked.

He grinned ruefully in the darkness. "I couldn't say that I'm exactly yearnin' for grub," he returned, "though I ain't done any eatin' since mornin'. I reckon a rattler's bite ain't considered to help a man's appetite any."

He heard her laugh softly. "No," she returned; "I wouldn't recommend it."

He tried again to see her, but could not, and so he relaxed and turned his gaze on the sky. But presently he felt her hand on his shoulder, and then her voice, as she spoke firmly.

"You can't lie here all night," she said. "You would be worse in the morning. And it is impossible for you to travel to-night. I am going to help you to get into the house. You can lean your weight on my shoulder."

He struggled to an erect position and made out her slender figure in the dim light from the window. He would have been afraid of crushing her could he have been induced to accept her advice. He got to his uninjured foot and began to hop toward the door, but she was beside him instantly protesting.

"Stop!" she commanded firmly. "If you do that it will be the worse for you. Put your hand on my shoulder!"

In the darkness he could see her eyes flash with determination, and so without further objection he placed a hand lightly on her shoulder, and in this manner they made their way through the door and into the cabin. Once inside the door he halted, blinking at the light and undecided. But she promptly led him toward another door, into a room containing a bed. She led him to the bedside and stood near him after he had sunk down upon it.

"You are to sleep here to-night," she said. "To-morrow, if you are considerably better, I may allow you to travel." She went out, returning immediately with a small bottle containing medicine. "If you feel worse during the night," she directed, "you must take a spoonful from that bottle. If you think you need anything else, don't hesitate to call. I shall be in the next room."

He started to voice his thanks, but she cut him short with a laugh. "Good-night," she said. Then she went out and closed the door after her.

He awoke several times during the night and each time took a taste of the medicine in the bottle. But shortly after midnight he fell into a heavy sleep, from which he did not awaken until the dawn had come. He lay quiet for a long time, until he heard steps in the kitchen, and then he rose and went to the door, throwing it open and standing on the threshold.

She was standing near the table, a coffee pot in her hand. Her eyes widened as she saw him.

"Oh!" she exclaimed. "You are very much better!"

He smiled. "I'm thankin' you for it, ma'am," he returned. "I cert'nly wouldn't have been feelin' anything if I hadn't met you when I did."

She put the coffee pot down and looked gravely at him.

"You were in very bad shape when you came," she admitted. "There was a time when I thought my remedies would not pull you through. They would not had you come five minutes later."

He had no reply to make to this, and he stood there silent, until she poured coffee into a cup, arranged some dishes, and then invited him to sit at the table.

He needed no second invitation, for he had been twenty-four hours without food. And he had little excuse to complain of the quality of the food that was set before him. He ate in silence and when he had finished he turned away from the table to see the girl dragging a rocking chair out upon the porch. She returned immediately, smiling at him.

"Your chair is ready," she said. "I think you had better not exert yourself very much to-day."

"Why, ma'am," he expostulated, "I'm feelin' right well. I reckon I could be travelin' now. I ain't used to bein' babied this way."

"I don't think you are being 'babied,'" she returned a trifle coldly. "I don't think that I would waste any time with anyone if I thought it wasn't necessary. I am merely telling you to remain for your own good. Of course, if you wish to disregard my advice you may do so."

He smiled with a frank embarrassment and limped toward the door. "Why, ma'am," he said regretfully as he reached the door, "I cert'nly don't want to do anything which you think ain't right, after what you've done for me. I don't want to belittle you, an' I think that when I said that I might have been gassin' a little. But I thought mebbe I'd been enough trouble already."

It was not entirely the confession itself, but the self-accusing tone in which it had been uttered that brought a smile to her face.

"All the same," she said, "you are to do as I tell you."

He smiled as he dropped into the chair on the porch. It was an odd experience for him. Never before in his life had anyone adopted toward him an air of even partial proprietorship. He had been accustomed to having people—always men—meet him upon a basis of equality, and if a man had adopted toward him the tone that she had employed there would have been an instant severing of diplomatic relations and a beginning of hostilities.

But this situation was odd—a woman had ordered him to do a certain thing and he was obeying, realizing that in doing so he was violating a principle, though conscious of a strange satisfaction. He knew that he had promised the Two Diamond manager, and he was convinced that, in spite of the pain in his foot, he was well enough to ride. But he was not going to ride; her command had settled that.

For a long time he sat in the chair, looking out over a great stretch of flat country which was rimmed on three sides by a fringe of low hills, and behind him by the cottonwood. The sun had been up long; it was swimming above the rim of distant hills—a ball of molten silver in a shimmering white blur. The cabin was set squarely in the center of a big clearing, and about an eighth of a mile behind him was a river—the river that he had been following when he had been bitten by the rattler.

He knew from the location of the cabin that he had not gone very far out of his way; that a ride of an eighth of a mile would bring him to the Two Diamond trail. And he could not be very far from the Two Diamond. Yet because of an order, issued by a girl, he was doomed to delay his appearance at the ranch.

He had seen no man about the cabin. Did the girl live here alone? He was convinced that no woman could long survive the solitude of this great waste of country—some man—a brother or a husband—must share the cabin with her. Several times he caught himself hoping that if there was a man here it might be a brother, or even a distant relative. The thought that she might have a husband aroused in him a sensation of vague disquiet.

He heard her moving about in the cabin, heard the rattle of dishes, the swish of a broom on the rough floor. And then presently she came out, dragging another rocker. Then she re-entered the cabin, returning with a strip of striped cloth and a sewing basket. She seated herself in the chair, placed the basket in her lap, and with a half smile on her face began to ply the needle. He lay back contentedly and watched her.

Hers was a lithe, vigorous figure in a white apron and a checkered dress of some soft material. She wore no collar; her sleeves were shoved up above the elbows, revealing a pair of slightly browned hands and white, rounded arms. Her eyes were brown as her hair—the latter in a tumble of graceful disorder. Through half closed eyes he was appraising her in a riot of admiration that threatened completely to bias his judgment. And yet women had interested him very little.

Perhaps that was because he had never seen a woman like this one. The women that he had known had been those of the plains-town—the unfortunates who through circumstances or inclination had been drawn into the maelstrom of cow-country vice, and who, while they may have found flattery, were never objects of honest admiration or respect.

He had known this young woman only a few hours, and yet he knew that with her he could not adopt the easy, matter-of-fact intimacy that had answered with the other women he had known. In fact, the desire to look upon her in this light never entered his mind. Instead, he was filled with a deep admiration for her—an admiration in which there was a profound respect.

"I expect you must know your business, ma'am," he said, after watching her for a few minutes. "An' I'm mighty glad that you do. Most women would have been pretty nearly flustered over a snake bite."

"Why," she returned, without looking up, but exhibiting a little embarrassment, which betrayed itself in a slight flush, "I really think that

I was a little excited—especially when you came riding up to the porch." She thought of his words, when, looking at her accusingly, he had told her that she was "a hell of a snake," and the flush grew, suffusing her face. This of course he had not known and never would know, but the words had caused her many smiles during the night.

"You didn't show it much," he observed. "You must have took right a-hold. Some women would have gone clean off the handle. They wouldn't have been able to do anything."

Her lips twitched, but she still gave her attention to her sewing, treating his talk with a mild interest.

"There is nothing about a snake bite to become excited over. That is, if treatment is applied in time. In your case the tourniquet kept the poison from getting very far into your system. If you hadn't thought of that it might have gone very hard with you."

"That rope around my leg wouldn't have done me a bit of good though, ma'am, if I hadn't stumbled onto your cabin. I don't know when seein' a woman has pleased me more."

She smiled enigmatically, her eyelashes flickering slightly. But she did not answer.

Until noon she sewed, and he lay lazily back in the chair, watching her sometimes, sometimes looking at the country around him. They talked very little. Once, when he had been looking at her for a long time, she suddenly raised her eyes and they met his fairly. Both smiled, but he saw a blush mantle her cheeks.

At noon she rose and entered the cabin. A little later she called to him, telling him that dinner was ready. He washed from the tin basin that stood on the bench just outside the door, and entering sat at the table and ate heartily.

After dinner he did not see her again for a time, and becoming wearied of the chair he set out on a short excursion to the river. When he returned she was seated on the porch and looked up at him with a demure smile.

"You will be quite active by to-morrow," she said.

"I ain't feelin' exactly lazy now," he returned, showing a surprising agility in reaching his chair.

When the sun began to swim low over the hills, he looked at her with a curiously grim smile.

"I reckon that rattler was fooled last night," he said. "But if foolin' him had been left to me I expect I'd have made a bad job of it. But I'm thinkin' that he done his little old dyin' when the sun went down last night. An' I'm still here. An' I'll keep right on, usin' his brothers an' sisters for targets—when I think that I'm needin' practice."

"Then you killed the snake?"

"Why sure, ma'am. I wasn't figgerin' to let that rattler go a-fannin' right on to hook someone else. That'd be encouragin' his trade."

She laughed, evidently pleased over his earnestness. "Oh, I see," she said. "Then you were not angry merely because he bit you? You killed him to keep him from attacking other persons?"

He smiled. "I sure was some angry," he returned. "An' I reckon that just at the time I wasn't thinkin' much about other people. I was havin' plenty to keep me busy."

"But you killed him. How?"

"Why I shot him, ma'am. Was you thinkin' that I beat him to death with somethin'?"

Her lips twitched again, the corners turning suggestively inward. But now he caught her looking at his guns. She looked from them to his face. "All cowboys do not carry two guns," she said suddenly.

He looked gravely at her. "Well, no, ma'am, they don't. There's some that claim carryin' two guns is clumsy. But there's been times when I found them right convenient."

She fell silent now, regarding her sewing. A quizzical smile had reached his face. This exchange of talk had developed the fact that she was a stranger to the country. No Western girl would have made her remark about the guns.

He did not know whether or not he was pleased over the discovery. Certain subtle signs about her had warned him in the beginning that she was different from the other women of his acquaintance, but he had not thought of her being a stranger here, of her coming here from some other section of the country—the East, for instance.

Her being from the East would account for many things. First, it would make plain to him why she had smiled several times during their talks, over things in which he had been able to see no humor. Then it would answer the question that had formed in his mind concerning the fluency of her speech. Western girls that he had met had not attained that ease and poise which he saw was hers so naturally. Yet in spite of this accomplishment she was none the less a woman—demure eyed, ready to blush and become confused as easily as a Western woman. Assured of this, he dropped the slight constraint which up till now had been plain in his voice, and an inward humor seemed to draw the corners of his mouth slightly downward.

"I reckon that folks where you come from don't wear guns at all, ma'am," he said slowly.

She looked up quickly, surprised into meeting his gaze fairly. His eyes did not waver. She rocked vigorously, showing some embarrassment and giving undue attention to her sewing.

"How do you know that?" she questioned, raising her head and looking at him with suddenly defiant eyes. "I am not aware that I told you that I was a stranger here! Don't you think you are guessing now?"

His eyes narrowed cunningly. "I don't think I need to do any guessin', ma'am," he returned. "When a man sees a different girl, he don't have to guess none."

The "different" girl was regarding him with furtive glances, plainly embarrassed under his direct words. But there was much defiance in her eyes, as though she was aware of the trend of his words and was determined to outwit him.

"I think you must be a remarkable man," she said, with the faintest trace of mockery in her voice, "to be able to discover such a thing so quickly. Or perhaps it is the atmosphere—it is marvelous."

"I expect it ain't exactly marvelous," he returned, laboring with the last word. "When a girl acts different, a man is pretty apt to know it." He leaned forward a little, speaking earnestly. "I know that I'm talkin' pretty plain to you, ma'am," he went on. "But when a man has been bit by a rattler an' has sort of give up hope an' has had his life saved by a girl, he's to be excused if he feels that he's some acquainted with the girl. An' then when he finds that she's some different from the girls he's been used to seein', I don't see why he hadn't ought to take a lot of interest in her."

"Oh!" she exclaimed, her eyes drooping. And then, her eyes dancing as they shot a swift glance at him—"I should call that a pretty speech."

He reddened with embarrassment. "I expect you are laughin' at me now, ma'am," he said. "But I wasn't thinkin' to make any pretty speeches. I was tellin' you the truth."

She soberly plied her needle, and he sat back, watching her.

"I expect you are a stranger around here yourself," she said presently, her eyes covered with drooping lashes. "How do you know that you have any right to sit there and tell me that you take an interest in me? How do you know that I am not married?"

He was not disconcerted. He drawled slightly over his words when he answered.

"You wouldn't listen at me at all, ma'am; you cert'nly wouldn't stay an' listen to any speeches that you thought was pretty, if you was married," he said. Plainly, he had not lost faith in the virtue of woman.

"But if I did listen?" she questioned, her face crimson, though her eyes were still defiant.

He regarded her with pleased eyes. "I've been lookin' for a weddin' ring," he said.

She gave it up in confusion. "I don't know why I am talking this way to you," she said. "I expect it is because there isn't anything else to do. But you really are entertaining!" she declared, for a parting shot.

Once Ferguson had seen a band of traveling minstrels in Cimarron. Their jokes (of an ancient vintage) had taken well with the audience, for the latter had laughed. Ferguson remembered that a stranger had said that the minstrels were "entertaining." And now he was entertaining her. A shadow passed over his face; he looked down at his foot, with its white bandage so much in evidence. Then straight at her, his eyes grave and steady.

"I'm glad to have amused you, ma'am," he said. "An' now I reckon I'll be gettin' over to the Two Diamond. It can't be very far now."

"Five miles," she said shortly. She had dropped her sewing into her lap and sat motionless, regarding him with level eyes.

"Are you working for the Two Diamond?" she questioned.

"Lookin' for a job," he returned.

"Oh!" The exclamation struck him as rather expressionless. He looked at her.

"Do you know the Two Diamond folks?"

"Of course."

"Of course," he repeated, aware of the constraint in her voice. "I ought to have known. They're neighbors of your'n."

"They are not!" she suddenly flashed back at him.

"Well, now," he returned slowly, puzzled, but knowing that somehow he was getting things wrong, "I reckon there's a lot that I don't know."

"If you are going to work over at the Two Diamond," she said coldly, "you will know more than you do now. My—"

Evidently she was about to say something more, but a sound caught her ear and she rose, dropping her sewing to the chair. "My brother is coming," she said quietly. Standing near the door she caught Ferguson's swift glance.

"Then it ain't a husband after all," he said, pretending surprise.

CHAPTER V

THE MAN OF DRY BOTTOM

A young man rode around the corner of the cabin and halted his pony beside the porch, sitting quietly in the saddle and gazing inquiringly at the two. He was about Ferguson's age and, like the latter, he wore two heavy guns. There was about him, as he sat there sweeping a slow glance over the girl and the man, a certain atmosphere of deliberate certainty and quiet coldness that gave an impression of readiness for whatever might occur.

Ferguson's eyes lighted with satisfaction. The girl might be an Easterner, but the young man was plainly at home in this country. Nowhere, except in the West, could he have acquired the serene calm that shone out of his eyes; in no other part of the world could he have caught the easy assurance, the unstudied nonchalance, that seems the inherent birthright of the cowpuncher.

"Ben," said the girl, answering the young man's glance, "this man was bitten by a rattler. He came here, and I treated him. He says he was on his way over to the Two Diamond, for a job."

The young man opened his lips slightly. "Stafford hire you?" he asked.

"I'm hopin' he does," returned Ferguson.

The young man's lips drooped sneeringly. "I reckon you're wantin' a job mighty bad," he said.

Ferguson smiled. "Takin' your talk, you an' Stafford ain't very good friends," he returned.

The young man did not answer. He dismounted and led his pony to a small corral and then returned to the porch, carrying his saddle.

For an instant after the young man had left the porch to turn his pony into the corral Ferguson had kept his seat on the porch. But something in the young man's tone had brought him out of the chair, determined to accept no more of his hospitality. If the young man was no friend of Stafford, it followed that he could not feel well disposed to a puncher who had avowed that his purpose was to work for the Two Diamond manager.

Ferguson was on his feet, clinging to one of the slender porch posts, preparatory to stepping down to go to his pony, when the young woman came out. Her sharp exclamation halted him.

"You're not going now!" she said. "You have got to remain perfectly quiet until morning!"

The brother dropped his saddle to the porch floor, grinning mildly at Ferguson, "You don't need to be in a hurry," he said. "I was intending to run your horse into the corral. What I meant about Stafford don't apply to you." He looked up at his sister, still grinning. "I reckon he ain't got nothing to do with it?"

The young woman blushed. "I hope not," she said in a low voice.

"We're goin' to eat pretty soon," said the young man. "I reckon that rattler didn't take your appetite?"

Ferguson flushed. "It was plum rediculous, me bein' hooked by a rattler," he said. "An' I've lived among them so long."

"I reckon you let him get away?" questioned the young man evenly.

"If he's got away," returned Ferguson, his lips straightening with satisfaction, "he's a right smart snake."

He related the incident of the attack, ending with praises of the young woman's skill.

The young man smiled at the reference to his sister. "She's studied medicine—back East. Lately she's turned her hand to writin'. Come out here to get experience—local color, she calls it."

Ferguson sat back in his chair, quietly digesting this bit of information. Medicine and writing. What did she write? Love stories? Fairy tales? Romances? He had read several of these. Mostly they were absurd and impossible. Love stories, he thought, would be easy for her. For—he said, mentally estimating her—a woman ought to know more about love than a man. And as for anything being impossible in a love story. Why most anything could happen to people who are in love.

"Supper is ready," he heard her announce from within.

Ferguson preceded the young man at the tin wash basin, taking a fresh towel that the young woman offered him from the doorway. Then he followed the young man inside. The three took places at the table, and Ferguson was helped to a frugal, though wholesome meal.

The dusk had begun to fall while they were yet at the table, and the young woman arose, lighting a kerosene lamp and placing it on the table. By the time they had finished semi-darkness had settled. Ferguson followed the young man out to the chairs on the porch for a smoke.

They were scarcely seated when there was a clatter of hoofs, and a pony and rider came out of the shadow of the nearby cottonwood, approaching the cabin and halting beside the porch. The newcomer was a man of about thirty-five. The light of the kerosene lamp shone fairly in his face as he sat in the saddle, showing a pair of cold, steady eyes and thin, straight lips that were wreathed in a smile.

"I thought I'd ride over for a smoke an' a talk before goin' down the crick to where the outfit's workin'," he said to the young man. And now his eyes swept Ferguson's lank figure with a searching glance. "But I didn't know you was havin' company," he added. The second glance that he threw toward Ferguson was not friendly.

Ferguson's lips curled slightly under it. Each man had been measured by the other, and neither had found in the other anything to admire.

Ferguson's thoughts went rapidly back to Dry Bottom. He saw a man in the street, putting five bullets through a can that he had thrown into the air. He saw again the man's face as he had completed his exhibition—insolent, filled with a sneering triumph. He heard again this man's voice, as he himself had offered to eclipse his feat:—

"You runnin' sheep, stranger?"

The voice and face of the man who stood before him now were the voice and face of the man who had preceded him in the shooting match in Dry Bottom. His thoughts were interrupted by the voice of his host, explaining his presence.

"This here man was bit by a rattler this afternoon," the young man was saying. "He's layin' up here for to-night. Says he's reckonin' on gettin' a job over at the Two Diamond."

The man on the horse sneered. "Hell!" he said; "bit by a rattler!" He laughed insolently, pulling his pony's head around. "I reckon I'll be goin'," he said. "You'll nurse him so's he won't die?" He had struck the pony's flanks with the spurs and was gone into the shadows before either man on the porch could move. There was a short silence, while the two men listened to the beat of his pony's hoofs. Then Ferguson turned and spoke to the young man.

"You know him?" he questioned.

The young man smiled coldly. "Yep," he said; "he's range boss for the Two Diamond!"

CHAPTER VI

AT THE TWO DIAMOND

As Ferguson rode through the pure sunshine of the morning his thoughts kept going back to the little cabin in the flat—"Bear Flat," she had called it. Certain things troubled him—he, whose mind had been always untroubled—even through three months of idleness that had not been exactly attractive.

"She's cert'nly got nice eyes," he told himself confidentially, as he lingered slowly on his way; "an' she knows how to use them. She sure made me seem some breathless. An' no girl has ever done that. An' her hair is like"—he pondered long over this—"like—why, I reckon I didn't just ever see anything like it. An' the way she looked at me!"

A shadow crossed his face. "So she's a writer—an' she's studied medicine. I reckon I'd like it a heap better if she didn't monkey with none of them fool things. What business has a girl got to—" He suddenly laughed aloud. "Why I reckon I'm pretty near loco," he said, "to be ravin' about a girl like this. She ain't nothin' to me; she just done what any other girl would do if a man come to her place bit by a rattler."

He spurred his pony forward at a sharp lope. And now he found that his thoughts would go back to the moment of his departure from the cabin that morning. She had accompanied him to the door, after bandaging the ankle. Her brother had gone away an hour before.

"I'm thankin' you, ma'am," Ferguson said as he stood for a moment at the door. "I reckon I'd have had a bad time if it hadn't been for you."

"It was nothing," she returned.

He had hesitated—he still felt the thrill of doubt that had assailed him before he had taken the step that he knew was impertinent. "I'll be ridin' over here again, some day, if you don't mind," he said.

Her face reddened a trifle. "I'm sure brother would like to have you," she replied.

"I don't remember to have said that I was comin' over to see your brother," was his reply.

"But it would have to be he," she said, looking straight at him. "You couldn't come to see me unless I asked you."

And now he had spoken a certain word that had been troubling him. "Do you reckon that Two Diamond range boss comes over to see your brother?"

She frowned. "Of course!" she replied. "He is my brother's friend. But I—I despise him!"

Ferguson grinned broadly. "Well, now," he said, unable to keep his pleasure over her evident dislike of the Two Diamond man from showing in his eyes and voice, "that's cert'nly too bad. An' to think he's wastin' his time—ridin' over here."

She gazed at him with steady, unwavering eyes. He could still remember the challenge in them. "Be careful that you don't waste your time!" was her answer.

"I reckon I won't," was his reply, as he climbed into the saddle. "But I won't be comin' over here to see your brother!"

"Oh, dear!" she said, "I call that very brazen!"

But when he had spurred his pony down through the crossing of the river he had turned to glance back at her. And he had seen a smile on her face. As he rode now he went over this conversation many times, much pleased with his own boldness; more pleased because she had not seemed angry with him.

It was late in the morning when he caught sight of the Two Diamond ranch buildings, scattered over a great basin through which the river flowed. Half an hour later he rode up to the ranchhouse and met Stafford at the door of the office. The manager waved him inside.

"I'm two days late," said Ferguson, after he had taken a chair in the office. He related to Stafford the attack by the rattler. The latter showed some concern over the injury.

"I reckon you didn't do your own doctorin'?" he asked.

Ferguson told him of the girl. The manager's lips straightened. A grim humor shone from his eyes.

"You stayed there over night?" he questioned.

"I reckon I stayed there. It was in a cabin down at a place which I heard the girl say was called 'Bear Flat.' I didn't ketch the name of the man."

Stafford grinned coldly. "I reckon they didn't know what you was comin' over here for?"

"I didn't advertise," returned Ferguson quietly.

"If you had," declared Stafford, his eyes glinting with a cold amusement, "you would have found things plum lively. The man's name is Ben Radford. He's the man I'm hirin' you to put out of business!"

For all Stafford could see Ferguson did not move a muscle. Yet the news had shocked him; he could feel the blood surging rapidly through his veins. But the expression of his face was inscrutable.

"Well, now," he said, "that sure would have made things interestin'. An' so that's the man you think has been stealin' your cattle?" He looked steadily at the manager. "But I told you before that I wasn't doin' any shootin'."

"Correct," agreed the manager. "What I want you to do is to prove that Radford's the man. We can't do anything until we prove that he's been rustlin'. An' then—" He smiled grimly.

"You reckon to know the girl's name too?" inquired Ferguson.

"It's Mary," stated the manager. "I've heard Leviatt talk about her."

Ferguson contemplated the manager gravely. "An' you ain't sure that Radford's stealin' your cattle?"

Stafford filled and lighted his pipe. "I'm takin' Dave Leviatt's word for it," he said.

"Who's Leviatt?" queried Ferguson.

"My range boss," returned Stafford. "He's been ridin' sign on Radford an' says he's responsible for all the stock that we've been missin' in the last six months."

Ferguson rolled a cigarette. He lighted it and puffed for a moment in silence, the manager watching him.

"Back at Dry Bottom," said Ferguson presently, "there was a man shootin' at a can when I struck town. He put five bullets through the can. Was that your range boss?"

Stafford smiled. "That was Leviatt—my range boss," he returned. "We went over to Dry Bottom to get a gunfighter. We wanted a man who could shoot plum quick. He'd have to be quick, for Radford's lightnin' with a six. Leviatt said shootin' at a can would be a good way to find a man who could take Radford's measure—in case it was necessary," he added quickly.

Ferguson's face was a mask of immobility. "Where's Leviatt now?" he questioned.

"Up the Ute with the outfit."

"How far up?"

"Thirty miles."

Ferguson's eyelashes flickered. "Has Leviatt been here lately?" he questioned.

"Not since the day before yesterday."

"When you expectin' him back?"

"The boys'll be comin' back in a week. He'll likely come along with them."

"U—um. You're giving me a free hand?"

"Of course."

Ferguson lounged to the door. "I'm lookin' around a little," he said, "to kind of size up things. I don't want you to put me with the outfit. That strike you right?"

"I'm hirin' you to do a certain thing," returned Stafford. "I ain't tellin' you how it ought to be done. You've got till the fall roundup to do it."

Ferguson nodded. He went to the corral fence, unhitched his pony, and rode out on the plains toward the river. Stafford watched him until he was a mere dot on the horizon. Then he smiled with satisfaction.

"I kind of like that guy," he said, commenting mentally. "There ain't no show work to him, but he's business."

CHAPTER VII

THE MEASURE OF A MAN

During the week following Ferguson's arrival at the Two Diamond ranch Stafford saw very little of him. Mornings saw him proceed to the corral, catch up his pony, mount, and depart. He returned with the dusk. Several times, from his office window, Stafford had seen him ride away in the moonlight.

Ferguson did his own cooking, for the cook had accompanied the wagon outfit down the river. Stafford did not seek out the new man with instructions or advice; the work Ferguson was engaged in he must do alone, for if complications should happen to arise it was the manager's business to know nothing.

The Two Diamond ranch was not unlike many others that dotted the grass plains of the Territory. The interminable miles that separated Stafford from the nearest, did not prevent him from referring to that particular owner as "neighbor", for distances were thus determined—and distances thus determined were nearly always inaccurate. The traveler inquiring for his destination was expected to discover it somewhere in the unknown distance.

The Two Diamond ranch had the enviable reputation of being "slick"—which meant that Stafford was industrious and thrifty and that his ranch bore an appearance of unusual neatness. For example, Stafford believed in the science of irrigation. A fence skirted his buildings, another ran around a large area of good grass, forming a pasture for his horses.

His buildings were attractive, even though rough, for they revealed evidence of continued care. His ranchhouse boasted a sloped roof and paved galleries.

A garden in the rear was but another instance of Stafford's industry. He had cattle that were given extraordinary care because they were "milkers," for in his youth Stafford had lived on a farm and he remembered days when his father had sent him out into the meadow to drive the cows home for the milking. There were many other things that Stafford had not forgotten, for chickens scratched promiscuously about the ranch yard, occasionally trespassing into the sacred precincts of the garden and the flower beds. His horses were properly stabled during the cold, raw days that came inevitably; his men had little to complain of, and there was a general atmosphere of prosperity over the entire ranch.

But of late there had been little contentment for the Two Diamond manager. For six months cattle thieves had been at work on his stock. The result of the spring round-up had been far from satisfactory. He knew of the existence of nesters in the vicinity; one of them—Radford—he had suspected upon evidence submitted by the range boss. Radford had been warned to vacate Bear Flat, but the warning had been disregarded.

But one other course was left, and Stafford had adopted that. There had been no hesitancy on the manager's part; he must protect the Two Diamond property. Sentiment had no place in the situation whatever. Therefore toward Ferguson's movements Stafford adopted an air of studied indifference, not doubting, from what he had seen of the man, that he would eventually ride in and report that the work which he had been hired to do was finished.

Toward the latter end of the week the wagon outfit straggled in. They came in singly, in twos and threes, bronzed, hardy, seasoned young men, taciturn, serene eyed, capable. They continued to come until there were twenty-seven of them. Later in the day came the wagon and the remuda.

From a period of calm and inaction the ranch now awoke to life and movement. The bunkhouse was scrubbed;—"swabbed" in the vernacular of the cowboys; the scant bedding was "cured" in the white sunlight; and the cook was adjured to extend himself in the preparation of "chuck" (meaning food) to repay the men for the lack of good things during a fortnight on the open range with the wagon.

At dusk on the first day in Rope Jones, a tall, lithe young puncher, whose spare moments were passed in breaking the wild horses that occasionally found their way to the Two Diamond, was oiling his saddle leathers. Sitting on a bench outside the bunkhouse he became aware of Stafford standing near.

"Leviatt come in?" queried the manager.

The puncher grinned. "Nope. Last I seen of Dave he was hittin' the breeze toward Bear Flat. Said he'd be in later." He lowered his voice significantly. "Reckon that Radford girl is botherin' Dave a heap."

Stafford smiled coldly and was about to answer when he saw Ferguson dropping from his pony at the corral gate. Following Stafford's gaze, Rope also observed Ferguson. He looked up at Stafford.

"New man?" he questioned.

Stafford nodded. He had invented a plausible story for the presence of Ferguson. Sooner or later the boys would have noticed the latter's absence from the outfit. Therefore if he advanced his story now there would be less conjecture later.

"You boys have got enough to do," he said, still watching Ferguson. "I've hired this man to look up strays. I reckon he c'n put in a heap of time at it."

Rope shot a swift glance upward at the manager's back. Then he grinned furtively. "Two-gun," he observed quietly; "with the bottoms of his holsters tied down. I reckon your stray-man ain't for to be monkeyed with."

But Stafford had told his story and knew that within a very little time Rope would be telling it to the other men. So without answering he walked toward the ranchhouse. Before he reached it he saw Leviatt unsaddling at the corral gate.

When Ferguson, with his saddle on his shoulder, on his way to place it on its accustomed peg in the lean-to adjoining the bunkhouse, passed Rope, it was by the merest accident that one of the stirrups caught the cinch buckle of Rope's saddle. Not observing the tangle, Ferguson continued on his way. He halted when he felt the stirrup strap drag, turning half around to see what was wrong. He smiled broadly at Rope.

"You reckon them saddles are acquainted?" he said.

Rope deftly untangled them. "I ain't thinkin' they're relations," he returned, grinning up at Ferguson. "Leastways I never knowed a 'double cinch' an' a 'center fire' to git real chummy."

"I reckon you're right," returned Ferguson, his eyes gleaming cordially; "an' I've knowed men to lose their tempers discussin' whether a center fire or a double cinch was the most satisfyin'."

"Some men is plum fools," returned Rope, surveying Ferguson with narrow, pleased eyes. "You didn't observe that the saddles rode any easier after the argument than before?"

"I didn't observe. But mebbe the men was more satisfied. Let a man argue that somethin' he's got is better'n somethin' that another fellow's got an' he falls right in love with his own—an' goes right on fallin' in love with it. Nothin' c'n ever change his mind after an argument."

"I know a man who's been studyin' human nature," observed Rope, grinning.

"An' not wastin' his time arguin' fool questions," added Ferguson.

"You sure ain't plum greenhorn," declared Rope admiringly.

"Thank yu'," smiled Ferguson; "I wasn't lookin' to see whether you'd cut your eye-teeth either."

"Well, now," remarked Rope, rising and shouldering his saddle, "you've almost convinced me that a double cinch ain't a bad saddle. Seems to make a man plum good humored."

"When a man's hungry an' right close to the place where he's goin' to feed," said Ferguson gravely, "he hadn't ought to bother his head about nothin'."

"You're settin' at my right hand at the table," remarked Rope, delighted with his new friend.

Several of the men were already at the washtrough when Rope and Ferguson reached there. The method by which they performed their ablutions was not delicate, but it was thorough. And when the dust had been removed their faces shone with the dusky health-bloom that told of their hard, healthy method of living. Men of various ages were there—grizzled riders who saw the world through the introspective eye of experience; young men with their enthusiasms, their impulses; middle-aged men who had seen much of life—enough to be able to face the future with unshaken complacence; but all bronzed, clear-eyed, self-reliant, unafraid.

When Ferguson and Rope entered the bunkhouse many of the men were already seated. Ferguson and Rope took places at one end of the long table and began eating. No niceties of the conventions were observed here; the men ate each according to his whim and were immune from criticism. Table etiquette was a thing that would have spoiled their joy of eating. Theirs was a primitive country; their occupation primitive; their manner of living no less so. They concerned themselves very little with the customs of a world of which they heard very little.

Nor did they bolt their food silently—as has been recorded of them by men who knew them little. If they did eat rapidly it was because the ravening hunger of a healthy stomach demanded instant attention. And they did not overeat. Epicurus would have marveled at the simplicity of their food. Conversation was mingled with every mouthful.

At one end of the table sat an empty plate, with no man on the bench before it. This was the place reserved for Leviatt, the range boss. Next to this place on the right was seated a goodlooking young puncher, whose age might have been estimated at twenty-three. "Skinny" they called him because of his exceeding slenderness. At the moment Ferguson settled into his seat the young man was filling the room with rapid talk. This talk had been inconsequential and concerned only those small details about which we bother during our leisure. But now his talk veered and he was suddenly telling something that gave promise of consecutiveness and universal interest. Other voices died away as his arose.

"Leviatt ain't the only one," he was saying. "She ain't made no exception with any of the outfit. To my knowin' there's been Lon Dexter, Soapy, Clem Miller, Lazy, Wrinkles—an' myself," he admitted, reddening, "been notified that we was mavericks an' needed our ears marked. An' now comes Leviatt a-fannin' right on to get his'n. An' I reckon he'll get it."

"You ain't tellin' what she said when she give you your'n," said a voice.

There was a laugh, through which the youth emerged smiling broadly.

"No," he said, "I ain't tellin'. But she told Soapy here that she was lookin' for local color. Wanted to know if he was it. Since then Soapy's been using a right smart lot of soap, tryin' to rub some color into his face."

Color was in Soapy's face now. He sat directly opposite the slender youth and his cheeks were crimson.

"I reckon if you'd keep to the truth—" he began. But Skinny has passed on to the next.

"An' there's Dexter. Lon's been awful quiet since she told him he had a picturesque name. Said it'd do for to put into a book which she's goin' to write, but when it come to choosin' a husband she'd prefer to tie up to a commoner name. An' so Lon didn't graze on that range no more."

"This country's goin' plum to—" sneered Dexter. But a laugh silenced him. And the youth continued.

"It might have been fixed up for Lazy," he went on, "only when she found out his name was Lazy, she wanted to know right off if he could support a wife—providin' he got one. He said he reckoned he could, an' she told him he could experiment on some other woman. An' now Lazy'll have to look around quite a spell before he'll get another chancst. I'd call that bein' in mighty poor luck."

Lazy was giving his undivided attention to his plate.

"An' she come right out an' told Wrinkles he was too old; that when she was thinkin' of gettin' wedded to some old monolith she'd send word to Egypt, where they keep 'em in stock. Beats me where she gets all them words."

"Told me she'd studied her dictionary," said a man who sat near Ferguson.

The young man grinned. "Well, I swear if I didn't come near forgettin' Clem Miller!" he said. "If you hadn't spoke up then, I reckon you wouldn't have been in on this deal. An' so she told you she'd studied her dictionary! Now, I'd call that news. Some one'd been tellin' me that she'd asked you the meanin' of the word 'evaporate.' An' when you couldn't tell her she told you to do it. Said that when you got home you might look up a dictionary an' then you'd know what she meant.

"An' now Leviatt's hangin' around over there," continued the youth. "He's claimin' to be goin' to see Ben Radford, but I reckon he's got the same kind of sickness as the rest of us."

"An' you ain't sayin' a word about what she said to you," observed Miller. "She must have treated you awful gentle, seein' you won't tell."

"Well," returned the young man, "I ain't layin' it all out to you. But I'll tell you this much; she said she was goin' to make me one of the characters in that book she's writin'."

"Well, now," said Miller, "that's sure lettin' you down easy. Did she say what the character was goin' to be?"

"I reckon she did."

"An' now you're goin' to tell us boys?"

"An' now I'm goin' to tell you boys," returned Skinny. "But I reckon there's a drove of them characters here. You'll find them with every outfit, an' you'll know them chiefly by their bray an' their long, hairy ears."

The young man now smiled into his plate, while a chorus of laughter rose around him. In making himself appear as ridiculous a figure as the others, the young man had successfully extracted all the sting from his story and gained the applause of even those at whom he had struck.

But now a sound was heard outside, and Leviatt came into the room. He nodded shortly and took his place at the end of the table. A certain reserve came into the atmosphere of the room. No further reference was made to the subject that had aroused laughter, but several of the men snickered into their plates over the recollection of Leviatt's connection with the incident.

As the meal continued Leviatt's gaze wandered over the table, resting finally upon Ferguson. The range boss's face darkened.

Ferguson had seen Leviatt enter; several times during the course of the meal he felt Leviatt looking at him. Once, toward the end, his glance met the range boss's fairly. Leviatt's eyes glittered evilly; Ferguson's lips curled with a slight contempt.

And yet these men had met but twice before. A man meets another in North America—in the Antipodes. He looks upon him, meets his eye, and instantly has won a friend or made an enemy. Perhaps this will always be true of men. Certainly it was true of Ferguson and the range boss.

What force was at work in Leviatt when in Dry Bottom he had insulted Ferguson? Whatever the force, it had told him that the steady-eyed, deliberate gun-man was henceforth to be an enemy. Enmity, hatred, evil intent, shone out of his eyes as they met Ferguson's.

Beyond the slight curl of the lips the latter gave no indication of feeling. And after the exchange of glances he resumed eating, apparently unaware of Leviatt's existence.

Later, the men straggled from the bunkhouse, seeking the outdoors to smoke and talk. Upon the bench just outside the door several of the men sat; others stood at a little distance, or lounged in the doorway. With Rope, Ferguson had come out and was standing near the door, talking.

The talk was light, turning to trivial incidents of the day's work—things that are the monotony of the cowboy life.

Presently Leviatt came out and joined the group. He stood near Ferguson, mingling his voice with the others. For a little time the talk flowed easily and much laughter rose. Then suddenly above the good natured babble came a harsh word. Instantly the other voices ceased, and the men of the group centered their glances upon the range boss, for the harsh word had come from him. He had been talking to a man named Tucson and it was to the latter that he had now spoken.

"There's a heap of rattlers in this country," he had said.

Evidently the statement was irrelevant, for Tucson's glance at Leviatt's face was uncomprehending. But Leviatt did not wait for an answer.

"A man might easily claim to have been bit by one of them," he continued, his voice falling coldly.

The men of the group sat in a tense silence, trying to penetrate this mystery that had suddenly silenced their talk. Steady eyes searched out each face in an endeavor to discover the man at whom the range boss was talking. They did not discover him. Ferguson stood near Leviatt, an arm's length distant, his hands on his hips. Perhaps his eyes were more alert than those of the other men, his lips in a straighter line. But apparently he knew no more of this mystery than any of the others.

And now Leviatt's voice rose again, insolent, carrying an unmistakable personal application.

"Stafford hires a stray-man," he said, sneering. "This man claims to have been bit by a rattler an' lays up over night in Ben Radford's cabin—makin' love to Mary Radford."

Ferguson turned his head slightly, surveying the range boss with a cold, alert eye.

"A little while ago," he said evenly, "I heard a man inside tellin' about some of the boys learnin' their lessons from a girl over on Bear Flat. I reckon, Leviatt, that you've been over there to learn your'n. An' now you've got to let these boys know—!"

Just a rustle it was—a snake-like motion. And then Ferguson's gun was out; its cold muzzle pressed deep into the pit of Leviatt's stomach, and Ferguson's left hand was pinning Leviatt's right to his side, the range boss's hand still wrapped around the butt of his half-drawn weapon. Then came Ferguson's voice again, dry, filled with a quiet earnestness:

"I ain't goin' to hurt you—you're still tenderfoot with a gun. I just wanted to show these boys that you're a false alarm. I reckon they know that now."

Leviatt sneered. There was a movement behind Ferguson. Tucson's gun was half way out of its holster. And then arose Rope's voice as his weapon came out and menaced Tucson.

"Three in this game would make it odd, Tucson," he said quietly. "If there's goin' to be any shootin', let's have an even break, anyway."

Tucson's hand fell away from his holster; he stepped back toward the door, away from the range boss and Ferguson.

Leviatt's face had crimsoned. "Mebbe I was runnin' a little bit wild—" he began.

"That's comin' down right handsome," said Ferguson.

He sheathed his gun and deliberately turned his back on Leviatt. The latter stood silent for a moment, his face gradually paling. Then he turned to where Tucson had taken himself and with his friend entered the bunkhouse. In an instant the old talk arose and the laughter, but many furtive glances swept Ferguson as he stood, talking quietly with Rope.

The following morning Stafford came upon Rope while the latter was throwing the saddle on his pony down at the corral gate.

"I heard something about some trouble between Dave Leviatt an' the new stray-man," said Stafford. "I reckon it wasn't serious?"

Rope turned a grave eye upon the manager. "Shucks," he returned, "I reckon it wasn't nothin' serious. Only," he continued with twitching lips, "Dave was takin' the stray-man's measure."

Stafford smiled grimly. "How did the stray-man measure up?" he inquired, a smile working at the corners of his mouth. "I reckon he wasn't none shy?"

Rope grinned, admiration glinting his eyes. "He's sure man's size," he returned, giving his attention to the saddle cinch.

CHAPTER VIII

THE FINDING OF THE ORPHAN

During the few first days of his connection with the Two Diamond Ferguson had reached the conclusion that he would do well to take plenty of time to inquire into the situation before attempting any move. He had now been at the Two Diamond for two weeks and he had not even seen Radford. Nor had he spoken half a dozen words with Stafford. The manager had observed certain signs that had convinced him that speech with the stray-man was unnecessary and futile. If he purposed to do anything he would do it in his own time and in his own way. Stafford mentally decided that the stray-man was "set in his ways."

The wagon outfit had departed,—this time down the river. Rope Jones had gone with the wagon, and therefore Ferguson was deprived of the companionship of a man who had unexpectedly taken a stand with him in his clash with Leviatt and for whom he had conceived a great liking.

With the wagon had gone Leviatt also. During the week that had elapsed between the clash at the bunkhouse and the departure of the wagon the range boss had given no sign that he knew of the existence of Ferguson. Nor had he intimated by word or sign that he meditated revenge upon Rope because of the latter's championship of the stray-man. If he had any such intention he concealed it with consummate skill. He treated Rope with a politeness that drew smiles to the faces of the men. But Ferguson saw in this politeness a subtleness of purpose that gave him additional light on the range boss's character. A man who held his vengeance at his finger tips would have taken pains to show Rope that he might expect no mercy. Had Leviatt revealed an open antagonism to Rope, the latter might have known what to expect when at last the two men would reach the open range and the puncher be under the direct domination of the man he had offended.

There were many ways in which a petty vengeance might be gratified. It was within the range boss's power to make life nearly unbearable for the puncher. If he did this it would of course be an unworthy vengeance, and Ferguson had little doubt that any vengeance meditated by Leviatt would not be petty.

Ferguson went his own way, deeply thoughtful. He was taking his time. Certain things were puzzling him. Where did Leviatt stand in this rustling business? That was part of the mystery. Stafford had told him that he had Leviatt's word that Radford was the thief who had been stealing the Two Diamond cattle. Stafford had said also that it had been Leviatt who had suggested employing a gunfighter—had even gone to Dry Bottom with the manager for the purpose of finding one. And now that one had been employed Leviatt had become suddenly antagonistic to him.

And Leviatt was in the habit of visiting the Radford cabin. Of course he might be doing this for the purpose of spying upon Ben Radford, but if that were the case why had he shown so venomous when he had seen Ferguson sitting on the porch on the evening of the day after the latter had been bitten by the rattler?

Mary Radford had told him that Leviatt was her brother's friend. If he was a friend of the brother why had he suggested that Stafford employ a gunfighter to shoot him? Here was more mystery.

On a day soon after the departure of the wagon outfit he rode away through the afternoon sunshine. Not long did his thoughts dwell upon the mystery of the range boss and Ben Radford. He kept seeing a young woman kneeling in front of him, bathing and binding his foot. Scraps of a conversation that he had not forgotten revolved in his mind and brought smiles to his lips.

"She didn't need to act so plum serious when she told me that I didn't know that I had any right to set there an' make pretty speeches to her . . . She wouldn't need to ask me to stay at the cabin all night. I could have gone on to the Two Diamond. I reckon that snake bite wasn't so plum dangerous that I'd have died if I'd have rode a little while."

As he came out of a little gully a few miles up the river and rode along the crest of a ridge that rose above endless miles of plains, his thoughts went back to that first night in the bunkhouse when the outfit had come in from the range. Satisfaction glinted in his eyes.

"I reckon them boys didn't make good with her. An' I expect that some day Leviatt will find he's been wastin' his time."

He frowned at thought of Leviatt and unconsciously his spurs drove hard against the pony's flanks. The little animal sprang forward, tossing his head spiritedly. Ferguson grinned and patted its flank with a remorseful hand.

"Well, now, Mustard," he said, "I wasn't reckonin' on takin' my spite out on you. You don't expect I thought you was Leviatt." And he patted the flank again.

He rode down the long slope of the rise and struck the level, traveling at a slow lope through a shallow washout. The ground was broken and rocky here and the snake-like cactus caught at his stirrup leathers. A rattler warned from the shadow of some sage-brush and, remembering his previous experience, he paused long enough to shoot its head off.

"There," he said, surveying the shattered snake, "I reckon you ain't to blame for me bein' bit by your uncle or cousin, or somethin', but I ain't never goin' to be particular when I see one of your family swingin' their head that suggestive."

He rode on again, reloading his pistol. For a little time he traveled at a brisk pace and then he halted to breathe Mustard. Throwing one leg over the pommel, he turned half way around in the saddle and swept the plains with a casual glance.

He sat erect instantly, focusing his gaze upon a speck that loomed through a dust cloud some miles distant. For a time he watched the speck, his eyes narrowing. Finally he made out the speck to be a man on a pony.

"He's a-fannin' it some," he observed, shading his eyes with his hands; "hittin' up the breeze for fair." He meditated long, a critical smile reaching his lips.

"It's right warm to-day. Not just the kind of an atmosphere that a man ought to be runnin' his horse reckless in." He meditated again.

"How far would you say he's off, Mustard? Ten miles, I reckon you'd say if you was a knowin' horse."

The horseman had reached a slight ridge and for a moment he appeared on the crest of it, racing his pony toward the river. Then he suddenly disappeared.

Ferguson smiled coldly. Again his gaze swept the plains and the ridges about him. "I don't see nothin' that'd make a man ride like that in this heat," he said. "Where would he have come from?" He stared obliquely off at a deep gully almost hidden by an adjoining ridge.

"It's been pretty near an hour since I shot that snake. I didn't see no man about that time. If he was around here he must have heard my gun—an' sloped." He smiled and urged his pony about. "I reckon we'll go look around that gully a little, Mustard," he said.

Half an hour later he rode down into the gully. After going some little distance he came across a dead cow, lying close to an overhanging rock rim. A bullet hole in the cow's forehead told eloquently of the manner of her death.

Ferguson dismounted and laid a hand on her side. The body was still warm. A four-months' calf was nudging the mother with an inquisitive muzzle. Ferguson took a sharp glance at its ears and then drove it off to get a look at the brand. There was none.

"Sleeper," he said quietly. "With the Two Diamond ear-mark. Most range bosses make a mistake in not brandin' their calves. Seems as if they're trustin' to luck that rustlers won't work on them. I must have scared this one off."

He swung into the saddle, a queer light in his eyes. "Mustard, old boy, we're goin' to Bear Flat. Mebbe Radford's hangin' around there now. An' mebbe he ain't. But we're goin' to see."

But he halted a moment to bend a pitying glance at the calf.

"Poor little dogie," he said; "poor little orphan. Losin' your mother—just like a human bein'. I call that mean luck."

Then he was off, Mustard swinging in a steady lope down the gully and up toward the ridge that led to the river trail.

CHAPTER IX

WOULD YOU BE A "CHARACTER"?

The sun was still a shimmering white blur in the great arc of sky when Ferguson rode around the corner of the cabin in Bear Flat, halted his pony, and sat quietly in the saddle before the door. His rapid eye had already swept the horse corral, the sheds, and the stable. If the horseman that he had seen riding along the ridge had been Radford he would not arrive for quite a little while. Meantime, he would learn from Miss Radford what direction the young man had taken on leaving the cabin.

Ferguson was beginning to take an interest in this game. At the outset he had come prepared to carry out his contract. In his code of ethics it was not a crime to shoot a rustler. Experience had taught him that justice was to be secured only through drastic action. In the criminal category of the West the rustler took a place beside the horse thief and the man who shot from behind.

But before taking any action Ferguson must be convinced of the guilt of the man he was hunting, and nothing had yet occurred that would lead him to suspect Radford. He did not speculate on what course he would take should circumstances prove Radford to be the thief. Would the fact that he was Mary Radford's brother affect his decision? He preferred to answer that question when the time came—if it ever came. One thing was certain; he was not shooting anyone unless the provocation was great.

His voice was purposely loud when he called "Whoa, Mustard!" to his pony, but his eyes were not purposely bright and expectant as they tried to penetrate the semi-darkness of the interior of the cabin for a glimpse of Miss Radford.

He heard a movement presently, and she was at the door looking at him, her hands folded in her apron, her eyes wide with unmistakable pleasure.

"Why, I never expected to see you again!" she exclaimed.

She came out and stood near the edge of the porch, making a determined attempt to subdue the flutter of excitement that was revealed in a pair of very bright eyes and a tinge of deep color in her cheeks.

"Then I reckon you thought I had died, or stampeded out of this country?" he answered, grinning. "I told you I'd be comin' back here."

But the first surprise was over, and she very properly retired to the shelter of a demurely polite reserve.

"So you did!" she made reply. "You told me you were comin' over to see my brother. But he is not here now."

Had he been less wise he would have reminded her that it had been she who had told him that he might come to see her brother. But to reply thus would have discomfited her and perhaps have brought a sharp reply. He had no doubt that some of the other Two Diamond men had made similar mistakes, but not he. He smiled broadly. "Mebbe I did," he said; "sometimes I'm mighty careless in handlin' the truth. Mebbe I thought then that I'd come over to see your brother. But we have different thoughts at different times. You say your brother ain't here now?"

"He left early this morning to go down the river," she informed him. "He said he would be back before sun-down."

His eyes narrowed perceptibly. "Down" the river meant that Radford's trail led in the general direction of the spot where he had seen the fleeing horseman and the dead Two Diamond cow with her orphaned calf. Yet this proved nothing. Radford might easily have been miles away when the deed had been done. For the present there was nothing he could do, except to wait until Radford returned, to form whatever conclusions he might from the young man's appearance when he should find a Two

Diamond man at the cabin. But anxiety to see the brother was not the only reason that would keep him waiting.

He removed his hat and sat regarding it with a speculative eye. Miss Radford smiled knowingly.

"I expect I have been scarcely polite," she said. "Won't you get off your horse?"

"Why, yes," he responded, obeying promptly; "I expect Mustard's been doin' a lot of wonderin' why I didn't get off before."

If he had meant to imply that her invitation had been tardy he had hit the mark fairly, for Miss Radford nibbled her lips with suppressed mirth. The underplay of meaning was not the only subtleness of the speech, for the tone in which it had been uttered was rich in interrogation, as though its author, while realizing the pony's dimness of perception, half believed the animal had noticed Miss Radford's lapse of hospitality.

"I'm thinkin' you are laughin' at me again, ma'am," he said as he came to the edge of the porch and stood looking up at her, grinning.

"Do you think I am laughing?" she questioned, again biting her lips to keep them from twitching.

"No-o. I wouldn't say that you was laughin' with your lips—laughin' regular. But there's a heap of it inside of you—tryin' to get out."

"Don't you ever laugh inwardly?" she questioned.

He laughed frankly. "I expect there's times when I do."

"But you haven't lately?"

"Well, no, I reckon not."

"Not even when you thought your horse might have noticed that I had neglected to invite you off?"

"Did I think that?" he questioned.

"Of course you did."

"Well, now," he drawled. "An' so you took that much interest in what I was thinkin'! I reckon people who write must know a lot."

Her face expressed absolute surprise. "Why, who told you that I wrote?" she questioned.

"Nobody told me, ma'am. I just heard it. I heard a man tell another man that you had threatened to make him a character in a book you was writin'."

Her face was suddenly convulsed. "I imagine I know whom you mean," she said. "A young cowboy from the Two Diamond used to annoy me quite a little, until one day I discouraged him."

His smile grew broad at this answer. But he grew serious instantly.

"I don't think there is much to write about in this country, ma'am," he said.

"You don't? Why, I believe you are trying to discourage me!"

"I reckon you won't listen to me, ma'am, if you want to write. I've heard that anyone who writes is a special kind of a person an' they just can't help writin'—any more'n I can help comin' over here to see your brother. You see, they like it a heap."

They both laughed, she because of the clever way in which he had turned the conversation to his advantage; he through sheer delight. But she did purpose to allow him to dwell on the point he had raised, so she adroitly took up the thread where he had broken off to apply his similitude.

"Some of that is true," she returned, giving him a look on her own account; "especially about a writer loving his work. But I don't think one needs to be a 'special' kind of person. One must be merely a keen observer."

He shook his head doubtfully. "I see everything that goes on around me," he returned. "Most of the time I can tell pretty near what sort a man is by lookin' at his face and watching the way he moves. But I reckon I'd never make a writer. Times when I look at this country—at a nice sunset, for instance, or think what a big place this country is—I feel like sayin' somethin' about it; somethin' inside of me seems kind of breathless-like—kind of scarin' me. But I couldn't write about it."

She had felt it, too, and more than once had sat down with her pencil to transcribe her thoughts. She thought that it was not exactly fear, but an overpowering realization of her own atomity; a sort of cringing of the soul away from the utter vastness of the world; a growing consciousness of the unlimited bigness of things; an insight of the infinite power of God—the yearning of the soul for understanding of the mysteries of life and existence.

She could sympathize with him, for she knew exactly how he had felt. She turned and looked toward the distant mountains, behind which the sun was just then swimming—a great ball of shimmering gold, which threw off an effulgent expanse of yellow light that was slowly turning into saffron and violet as it met the shadows below the hills.

"Whoever saw such colors?" she asked suddenly, her face transfixed with sheer delight.

"It's cert'nly pretty, ma'am."

She clapped her hands. "It is magnificent!" she declared enthusiastically. She came closer to him and stretched an arm toward the mountains. "Look at that saffron shade which is just now blending with the streak of pearl striking the cleft between those hills! See the violet tinge that has come into that sea of orange, and the purple haze touching the snow-caps of the mountains. And now the flaming red, the deep yellow, the slate blue; and now that gauzy veil of lilac, rose, and amethyst, fading and dulling as the darker shadows rise from the valleys!"

Her flashing eyes sought Ferguson's. Twilight had suddenly come.

"It is the most beautiful country in the world!" she said positively.

He was regarding her with gravely humorous eyes. "It cert'nly is pretty, ma'am," he returned. "But you can't make a whole book out of one sunset."

Her eyes flashed. "No," she returned. "Nor can I make a whole book out of only one character. But I am going to try and draw a word picture of the West by writing of the things that I see. And I am going to try and have some real characters in it. I shall try to have them talk and act naturally."

She smiled suddenly and looked at him with a significant expression. "And the hero will not be an Easterner—to swagger through the pages of the book, scaring people into submission through the force of his compelling personality. He will be a cowboy who will do things after the manner of the country—a real, unaffected care-free puncher!"

"Have you got your eye on such a man?" he asked, assuring himself that he knew of no man who would fill the requirements she had named.

"I don't mind telling you that I have," she returned, looking straight at him.

It suddenly burst upon him. His face crimsoned. He felt like bolting. But he managed to grin, though she could see that the grin was forced.

"It's gettin' late, ma'am," he said, as he turned toward his pony. "I reckon I'll be gettin' back to the Two Diamond."

She laughed mockingly as he settled into the saddle. There was a clatter of hoofs from around the corner of the cabin.

"Wait!" she commanded. "Ben is coming!"

But there was a rush of wind that ruffled her apron, a clatter, and she could hear Mustard's hoofs pounding over the matted mesquite that carpeted the clearing. Ferguson had fled.

CHAPTER X

DISAPPEARANCE OF THE ORPHAN

During the night Ferguson had dreamed dreams. A girl with fluffy brown hair and mocking eyes had been the center of many mental pictures that had haunted him. He had seen her seated before him, rapidly plying a pencil. Once he imagined he had peered over her shoulder. He had seen a sketch of a puncher, upon which she appeared to be working, representing a man who looked very like himself. He could remember that he had been much surprised. Did writers draw the pictures that appeared in their books?

This puncher was sitting in a chair; one foot was bandaged. As he watched over the girl's shoulder he saw the deft pencil forming the outlines of another figure—a girl. As this sketch developed he saw that it was to represent Miss Radford herself. It was a clever pencil that the girl wielded, for the scene was strikingly real. He even caught subtle glances from her eyes. But as he looked the scene changed and the girl stood at the edge of the porch, her eyes mocking him. And then to his surprise she spoke. "I am going to put you into a book," she said.

Then he knew why she had tolerated him. He had grown hot and embarrassed. "You ain't goin' to put me in any book, ma'am," he had said. "You ain't givin' me a square deal. I wouldn't love no girl that would put me into a book."

He had seen a sudden scorn in her eyes. "Love!" she said, her lips curling. "Do you really believe that I would allow a puncher to make love to me?"

And then the scene had changed again, and he was shooting the head off a rattler. "I don't want you to love me!" he had declared to it. And then while the snake writhed he saw another head growing upon it, and a face. It was the face of Leviatt; and there was mockery in this face also. While he looked it spoke.

"You'll nurse him so's he won't die?" it had said.

When he awakened his blood was surging with a riotous anger. The dream was bothering him now, as he rode away from the ranchhouse toward the gully where he had found the dead Two Diamond cow. He had not reported the finding of the dead cow, intending to return the next morning to look the ground over and to fetch the "dogie" back to the home ranch. It would be time enough then to make a report of the occurrence to Stafford.

It was mid-morning when he finally reached the gully and rode down into it. He found the dead cow still there. He dismounted to drive away some crows that had gathered around the body. Then he noticed that the calf had disappeared. It had strayed, perhaps. A calf could not be depended upon to remain very long beside its dead mother, though he had known cases where they had. But if it had strayed it could not be very far away. He remounted his pony and loped down the gully, reaching the ridge presently and riding along this, searching the surrounding country with keen glances. He could see no signs of the calf. He came to a shelf-rock presently, beside which grew a tangled gnarl of scrub-oak brush. Something lay in the soft sand and he dismounted quickly and picked up a leather tobacco pouch. He examined this carefully. There were no marks on it to tell who might be the owner.

"A man who loses his tobacco in this country is mighty careless," he observed, smiling; "or in pretty much of a hurry."

He went close to the thicket, looking down at it, searching the sand with interest. Presently he made out the impression of a foot in a soft spot and, looking further, saw two furrows that might have been made by a man kneeling. He knelt in the furrows himself and with one hand parted the brush. He smiled grimly as, peering into the gully, he saw the dead Two Diamond cow on the opposite side.

He stepped abruptly away from the thicket and looked about him. A few yards back there was a deep depression in the ridge, fringed with a growth of nondescript weed. He approached this and peered into it. Quite recently a horse had been there. He could plainly see the hoof-prints—where the animal had pawed impatiently. He returned to the thicket, convinced.

"Some one was here yesterday when I was down there lookin' at that cow," he decided. "They was watchin' me. That man I seen ridin' that other ridge was with the one who was here. Now why didn't this man slope too?"

He stood erect, looking about him. Then he smiled.

"Why, it's awful plain," he said. "The man who was on this ridge was watchin'. He heard my gun go off, when I shot that snake. I reckon he figgered that if he tried to ride away on this ridge whoever'd done the shootin' would see him. An' so he didn't go. He stayed right here an' watched me when I rode up." He smiled. "There ain't no use lookin' for that dogie. The man that stayed here has run him off."

There was nothing left for Ferguson to do. He mounted and rode slowly along the ridge, examining the tobacco pouch. And then suddenly he discovered something that brought an interested light to his eyes. Beneath the greasy dirt on the leather he could make out the faint outlines of two letters. Time had almost obliterated these, but by moistening his fingers and rubbing the dirt from the leather he was able to trace them. They had been burned in, probably branded with a miniature iron.

"D. L," he spelled.

He rode on again, his lips straightening into serious lines.

He mentally catalogued the names he had heard since coming to the Two Diamond. None answered for the initials "D. L." It was evident that the pouch could belong to no one but Dave Leviatt. In that case what had Leviatt been doing on the ridge? Why, he had been watching the rustler, of course. In that case the man must be known to him. But what had become of the dogie? What would have been Leviatt's duty, after the departure of the rustlers? Obviously to drive the calf to the herd and report the occurrence to the manager.

Leviatt may have driven the calf to the herd, but assuredly he had not reported the occurrence to the manager, for he had not been in to the ranchhouse. Why not?

Ferguson pondered long over this, while his pony traveled the river trail toward the ranchhouse. Finally he smiled. Of course, if the man on the ridge had been Leviatt, he must have been there still when Ferguson came up, or he would not have been there to drive the Two Diamond calf to the herd after Ferguson had departed. In that case he must have seen Ferguson, and must be waiting for the latter to make the report to the manager. But what motive would he have in this?

Here was more mystery. Ferguson might have gone on indefinitely arranging motives, but none of them would have brought him near the truth.

He could, however, be sure of three things. Leviatt had seen the rustler and must know him; he had seen Ferguson, and knew that he knew that a rustler had been in the gully before him; and for some mysterious reason he had not reported to the manager. But Ferguson had one advantage that pleased him, even drew a grim smile to his lips as he rode on his way. Leviatt may have seen him near the dead Two Diamond cow, but he certainly was not aware that Ferguson knew he himself had been there during the time that the rustler had been at work.

Practically, of course, this knowledge would avail Ferguson little. Yet it was a good thing to know, for Leviatt must have some reason for secrecy, and if anything developed later Ferguson would know exactly where the range boss stood in the matter.

Determined to investigate as far as possible, he rode down the river for a few miles, finally reaching a broad plain where the cattle were feeding.

Some cowboys were scattered over this plain, and before riding very far Ferguson came upon Rope. The latter spurred close to him, grinning.

"I'm right glad to see you," said the puncher. "You've been keepin' yourself pretty scarce. Scared of another run-in with Leviatt?"

"Plum scared," returned Ferguson. "I reckon that man'll make me nervous—give him time."

"Yu' don't say?" grinned Rope. "I wasn't noticin' that you was worryin' about him."

"I'm right flustered," returned Ferguson. "Where's he now?"

"Gone down the crick—with Tucson."

Ferguson smoothed Mustard's mane. "Leviatt been with you right along?"

"He went up the crick yesterday," returned Rope, looking quickly at the stray-man.

"Went alone, I reckon?"

"With Tucson." Rope was trying to conceal his interest in these questions.

But apparently Ferguson's interest was only casual. He turned a quizzical eye upon Rope. "You an' Tucson gettin' along?" he questioned.

"Me an' him's of the same mind about one thing," returned Rope.

"Well, now." Ferguson's drawl was pregnant with humor. "You surprise me. An' so you an' him have agreed. I reckon you ain't willin' to tell me what you've agreed about?"

"I'm sure tellin'," grinned Rope. "Me an' him's each dead certain that the other's a low down horse thief."

The eyes of the two men met fairly. Both smiled.

"Then I reckon you an' Tucson are lovin' one another about as well as me an' Leviatt," observed Ferguson.

"There ain't a turrible lot of difference," agreed Rope.

"An' so Tucson's likin' you a heap," drawled Ferguson absently. He gravely contemplated the puncher. "I expect you was a long ways off yesterday when Leviatt an' Tucson come in from up the crick?" he asked.

"Not a turruble ways off," returned Rope. "I happened to have this end an' they passed right close to me. They clean forgot to speak."

"Well, now," said Ferguson. "That was sure careless of them. But I reckon they was busy at somethin' when they passed. In that case they wouldn't have time to speak. I've heard tell that some folks can't do more'n one thing at a time."

Rope laughed. "They was puttin' in a heap of their time tryin' to make me believe they didn't see me," he returned. "Otherwise they wasn't doin' anything."

"Shucks!" declared Ferguson heavily. "I reckon them men wouldn't go out of their way to drive a poor little dogie in off the range. They're that hard hearted."

"Correct," agreed Rope. "You ain't missin' them none there."

Ferguson smiled, urging his pony about. "I'm figgerin' on gettin' back to the Two Diamond," he said. He rode a few feet and then halted, looking back over his shoulder. "You ain't givin' Tucson no chancst to say you drawed first?" he warned.

Rope laughed grimly. "If there's any shootin' goin' on," he replied, "Tucson ain't goin' to say nothin' after it's over."

"Well, so-long," said Ferguson, urging his pony forward. He heard Rope's answer, and then rode on, deeply concerned over his discovery.

Leviatt and Tucson had ridden up the river the day before. They had returned empty handed. And so another link had been added to the chain of mystery. Where was the dogie?

CHAPTER XI

A TOUCH OF LOCAL COLOR

A few months before her first meeting with Ferguson, Mary Radford had come West with the avowed purpose of "absorbing enough local color for a Western novel." Friends in the East had encouraged her; an uncle (her only remaining relative, beside her brother) had assisted her. So she had come.

The uncle (under whose care she had been since the death of her mother, ten years before) had sent her to a medical college, determined to make her a finished physician. But Destiny had stepped in. Quite by accident Miss Radford had discovered that she could write, and the uncle's hope that she might one day grace the medical profession had gone glimmering—completely buried under a mass of experimental manuscript.

He professed to have still a ray of hope until after several of the magazines had accepted Mary's work. Then hope died and was succeeded by silent acquiescence and patient resignation. Having a knowledge of human nature far beyond that possessed by the average person, the uncle had realized that if Mary's inclination led to literature it was worse than useless to attempt to interest her in any other profession. Therefore, when she had announced her intention of going West he had interposed no objection; on the contrary had urged her to the venture. What might have been his attitude had not Ben Radford been already in the West is problematical. Very seldom do we decide a thing until it confronts us.

Mary Radford had been surprised at the West. From Ben's cabin in the flat she had made her first communion with this new world that she had worshipped at first sight. It was as though she had stepped out of an old world into one that was just experiencing the dawn of creation's first morning. At least so it had seemed to her on the morning she had first stepped outside her brother's cabin to view her first sunrise.

She had breathed the sweet, moisture-laden breezes that had seemed to almost steal over the flat where she had stood watching the shadows yield to the coming sun. The somber hills had become slowly outlined; the snow caps of the distant mountain peaks glinted with the brilliant shafts that struck them and reflected into the dark recesses below. Nature was king here and showed its power in a mysterious, though convincing manner.

In the evening there would come a change. Through rifts in the mountains descended the sun, spreading an effulgent expanse of yellow light—like burnished gold. In the shadows were reflected numerous colors, all quietly blended, making contrasts of perfect harmony. There were the sinuous buttes that bordered the opposite shore of the river—solemn sentinels guarding the beauty and purity of this virgin land. Near her were sloping hills, dotted with thorny cactus and other prickly plants, and now rose a bald rock spire with its suggestion of grim lonesomeness. In the southern and eastern distances were the plains, silent, vast, unending. It seemed she had come to dwell in a land deserted by some cyclopean race. Its magnificent, unchanging beauty had enthralled her.

She had not lacked company. She found that the Two Diamond punchers were eager to gain her friendship. Marvelous excuses were invented for their appearance at the cabin in the flat. She thought that Ben's friendship was valued above that of all other persons in the surrounding country.

But she found the punchers gentlemen. Though their conversation was unique and their idioms picturesque, they compared favorably with the men she had known in the East. Did they lack the subtleties, they made up for this by their unfailing deference. And they were never rude; their very bashfulness prevented that.

Through them she came to know much of many things. They contrived to acquaint her with the secretive peculiarities of the prairie dog, and—when she would listen with more than ordinary attention—they would loose their wonderful imaginations in the hope of continuing the conversation. Then it was that the subject under discussion would receive exhaustive, and altogether unnecessary, elucidation. The habits of the prairie-dog were not alone betrayed to the ears of the young lady. The sage-fowl's inherent weaknesses were paraded before her; the hoot of the owl was imitated with ludicrous solemnity; other fowl were described with wonderful attention to detail; and the inevitable rattlesnake was pointed out to her as a serpent whose chief occupation in life was that of posing in the shadow of the sage-brush as a target for the revolver of the cowpuncher.

The quaintness of the cowboy speech, his incomparable bashfulness, amused her, while she was strangely affected by his earnestness. She attended to the chickens and immediately her visitors became interested in them and fell to discussing them as though they had done nothing all their days but build hen-houses and runways. But she had them on botany. The flower beds were deep, unfathomable mysteries to them, and they stood afar while she cultivated the more difficult plants and encouraged the hardier to increased beauty.

But she had not been content to view this land of mystery from her brother's cabin. The dignity of nature had cast its thrall upon her. She was impressed with the sublimity of the climate, the wonderful sunshine, the crystal light of the days and the quiet peace and beauty of the nights. The lure of the plains had taken her upon long rides, and the cottonwood, filling a goodly portion of the flat, was the scene of many of her explorations.

The pony with which her brother had provided her was—Ben Radford declared—a shining example of sterling horse-honesty. She did not know that Ben knew horses quite as well as he knew men or she would not have allowed him to see the skeptical glance she had thrown over the drowsy-eyed beast that he saddled for her. But she was overjoyed at finding the pony all that her brother had said of it. The little animal was tireless, and often, after a trip over the plains, or to Dry Bottom to mail a letter, she would return by a roundabout trail.

Meanwhile the novel still remained unwritten. Perhaps she had not yet "absorbed" the "local color"; perhaps inspiration was tardy. At all events she had not written a word. But she was beginning to realize the possibilities; deep in her soul something was moving that would presently flow from her pen.

It would not be commonplace—that she knew. Real people would move among the pages of her book; real deeds would be done. And as the days passed she decided. She would write herself into her book; there would be the first real character. The story would revolve about her and another character—a male one—upon whom she had not decided—until the appearance of Ferguson. After he had come she was no longer undecided—she would make him the hero of her story.

The villain she had already met—in Leviatt. Something about this man was repellant. She already had a description of him in the note book that she always carried. Had Leviatt read the things she had written of him he would have discontinued his visits to the cabin.

Several of the Two Diamond punchers, also, were noted as being possible secondary characters. She had found them very amusing. But the hero would be the one character to whom she would devote the concentrated effort of her mind. She would make him live in the pages; a real, forceful magnetic human being that the reader would instantly admire. She would bare his soul to the reader; she would reveal his mental processes—not involved, but leading straight and true to—

But would she? Had she not so far discovered a certain craftiness in the character of the Two Diamond stray-man that would indicate subtlety of thought?

This knowledge had been growing gradually upon her since their second meeting, and it had become an obstacle that promised difficulties. Of course she could make Ferguson talk and act as she pleased—in the book. But if she wanted a real character she would have to portray him as he was. To do this would require study. Serious study of any character would inspire faithful delineation.

She gave much thought to him now, keeping this purpose in view. She questioned Ben concerning him, but was unable to gain satisfying information. He had been hired by Stafford, her brother told her, holding the position of stray-man.

"I've seen him once, down the other side of the cottonwood," the young man had said. "He ain't saying much to anyone. Seems to be a quiet sort—and deep. Pretty good sort though."

She was pleased over Ben's brief estimate of the stray-man. It vindicated her judgment. Besides, it showed that her brother was not averse to friendship with him.

Leviatt she saw with her brother often, and occasionally he came to the cabin. His attitude toward her was one of frank admiration, but he had received no encouragement. How could he know that he was going to be the villain in her book—soon to be written?

Shall we take a peep into that mysterious note book? Yes, for later we shall see much of it.

"Dave Leviatt," she had written in one place. "Age thirty-five. Tall, slender; walks with a slight stoop. One rather gets the impression that the stoop is a reflection of the man's nature, which seems vindictive and suggests a low cunning. His eyes are small, deep set, and glitter when he talks. But they are steady, and cold—almost merciless. One's thoughts go instantly to the tiger. I shall try to create that impression in the reader's mind."

In another place she had jotted this down: "I shouldn't want anyone killed in my book, but if I find this to be necessary Leviatt must do the murder. But I think it would be better to have him employ some other person to do it for him; that would give him just the character that would fit him best. I want to make him seem too cowardly—no, not cowardly, because I don't think he is a coward: but too cunning—to take chances of being caught."

Evidently she had been questioning Ben, for in another place she had written:

"Ferguson. I must remember this—all cowboys do not carry two guns. Ben does, because he says he is ambidextrous, shooting equally well with either hand. But he does not tie the bottoms of his holsters down, like Ferguson; he says some men do this, but usually they are men who are exceptionally rapid in getting their revolvers out and that tying down the bottoms of the holsters facilitates removing the weapons. They are accounted to be dangerous men.

"Ben says when a man is quick to shoot out here he is called a gun-man, and that if he carries two revolvers he is a two-gun man. Ben laughs at me when I speak of a 'revolver'; they are known merely as 'guns' out here. I must remember this. Ben says that though he likes Ferguson quite well, he is rather suspicious of him. He seems to be unable to understand why Stafford should employ a two-gun man to look up stray cows."

Below this appeared a brief reference to Ferguson.

"He is not a bit conceited—rather bashful, I should say. But embarrassment in him is attractive. No hero should be conceited. There is a wide difference between impertinence and frankness. Ferguson seems to speak frankly, but with a subtle shade. I think this is a very agreeable trait for a hero in a novel."

There followed more interesting scraps concerning Leviatt, which would have caused the range boss many bad moments. And there were interesting bits of description—jotted down when she became impressed with a particularly odd view of the country. But there were no more references to Ferguson. He—being the hero of her novel—must be studied thoroughly.

CHAPTER XII

THE STORY BEGINS

Miss Radford tied her pony to the trunk of a slender fir-balsam and climbed to the summit of a small hill. There were some trees, quite a bit of grass, some shrubbery, on the hill—and no snakes. She made sure of this before seating herself upon a little shelf of rock, near a tall cedar.

Half a mile down the river she could see a corner of Ben's cabin, a section of the corral fence, and one of the small outbuildings. Opposite the cabin, across the river, rose the buttes that met her eyes always when she came to the cabin door. This hill upon which she sat was one that she saw often, when in the evening, watching the setting sun, she followed its golden rays with her eyes. Many times, as the sun had gone slowly down into a rift of the mountains, she had seen the crest of this hill shimmering in a saffron light; the only spot in the flat that rose above the somber, oncoming shadows of the dusk.

From here, it seemed, began the rose veil that followed the broad saffron shaft that led straight to the mountains. Often, watching the beauty of the hill during the long sunset, she had felt a deep awe stirring her. Romance was here, and mystery; it was a spot favored by the Sun-Gods, who surrounded it with a glorious halo, lingeringly, reluctantly withdrawing as the long shadows of the twilight crept over the face of the world.

It was not her first visit to the hill. Many times she had come here, charmed with the beauty of the view, and during one of those visits she had decided that seated on the shelf rock on the summit of the hill she would write the first page of the book. It was for this purpose that she had now come.

After seating herself she opened a small handbag, producing therefrom many sheets of paper, a much-thumbed copy of Shakespeare, and a pencil. She was tempted to begin with a description of the particular bit of country upon which she looked, for long ago she had decided upon Bear Flat for the locale of the story. But she sat long nibbling at the end of the pencil, delaying the beginning for fear of being unable to do justice to it.

She began at length, making several false starts and beginning anew. Finally came a paragraph that remained. Evidently this was satisfactory, for another paragraph followed; and then another, and still another. Presently a complete page. Then she looked up with a long-drawn sigh of relief. The start had been made.

She had drawn a word picture of the flat; dwelling upon the solitude, the desolation, the vastness, the swimming sunlight, the absence of life and movement. But as she looked, critically comparing what she had written with the reality, there came a movement—a horseman had ridden into her picture. He had come down through a little gully that led into the flat and was loping his pony through the deep saccatone grass toward the cabin.

It couldn't be Ben. Ben had told her that he intended riding some thirty miles down the river and he couldn't be returning already. She leaned forward, watching intently, the story forgotten.

The rider kept steadily on for a quarter of an hour. Then he reached the clearing in which the cabin stood; she saw him ride through it and disappear. Five minutes later he reappeared, hesitated at the edge of the clearing and then urged his pony toward the hill upon which she sat. As he rode out of the shadows of the trees within an eighth of a mile of her the sunlight shone fairly upon the pony. She would have known Mustard among many other ponies.

She drew a sudden, deep breath and sat erect, tucking back some stray wisps of hair from her forehead. Did the rider see her?

For a moment it seemed that the answer would be negative, for he disappeared behind some dense shrubbery on the plain below and seemed to be on the point of passing the hill. But just at the edge of the shrubbery Mustard suddenly swerved and came directly toward her. Through the corners of her eyes she watched while Ferguson dismounted, tied Mustard close to her own animal, and stood a moment quietly regarding her.

"You want to look at the country all by yourself?" he inquired.

She pretended a start, looking down at him in apparent surprise.

"Why," she prevaricated, "I thought there was no one within miles of me!"

She saw his eyes flash in the sunlight. "Of course," he drawled, "there's such an awful darkness that no one could see a pony comin' across the flat. You think you'll be able to find your way home?"

She flushed guiltily and did not reply. She heard him clambering up over the loose stones, and presently he stood near her. She made a pretense of writing.

"Did you stop at the cabin?" she asked without looking up.

He regarded her with amused eyes, standing loosely, his arms folded, the fingers of his right hand pulling at his chin. "Did I stop?" he repeated. "I couldn't rightly say. Seems to me as though I did. You see, I didn't intend to, but I was ridin' down that way an' I thought I'd stop in an' have a talk with Ben."

"Oh!" Sometimes even a monosyllable is pregnant with mockery.

"But he wasn't there. Nobody was there. I wasn't reckonin' on everybody runnin' off."

She turned and looked straight at him. "Why," she said, "I shouldn't think our running away would surprise you. You see, you set us an example in running away the other day."

He knew instantly that she referred to his precipitate retreat on the night she had hinted that she intended putting him into her story. She shot another glance at him and saw his face redden with embarrassment, but he showed no intention of running now.

"I've been thinkin' of what you said," he returned. "You couldn't put me into no book. You don't know anything about me. You don't know what I think. Then how could you do it?"

"Of course," she returned, turning squarely around to him and speaking seriously, "the story will be fiction, and the plot will have no foundation in fact. But I shall be very careful to have my characters talk and act naturally. To do this I shall have to study the people whom I wish to characterize."

He was moved by an inward mirth. "You're still thinkin' of puttin' me into the book?" he questioned.

She nodded, smiling.

"Then," he said, very gravely, "you hadn't ought to have told me. You didn't show so clever there. Ain't you afraid that I'll go to actin' swelled? If I do that, you'd not have the character you wanted."

"I had thought of that, too," she returned seriously. "If you were that kind of a man I shouldn't want you in the book. How do you know that I haven't told you for the purpose of discovering if you would be affected in that manner?"

He scratched his head, contemplating her gravely. "I reckon you're travelin' too fast for me, ma'am," he said.

His expression of frank amusement was good to see. He stood before her, plainly ready to surrender. Absolutely boyish, he seemed to her—a grown-up boy to be sure, but with a boy's enthusiasms, impulses, and generosity. Yet in his eyes was something that told of maturity, of conscious power, of perfect trust in his ability to give a good account of himself, even in this country where these qualities constituted the chief rule of life.

A strange emotion stirred her, a sudden quickening of the pulse told her that something new had come into her life. She drew a deep, startled breath and felt her cheeks crimsoning. She swiftly turned her head and gazed out over the flat, leaving him standing there, scarcely comprehending her embarrassment.

"I reckon you've been writin' some of that book, ma'am," he said, seeing the papers lying on the rock beside her. "I don't see why you should want to write a Western story. Do folks in the East get interested in knowin' what's goin' on out here?"

She suddenly thought of herself. Had she found it interesting? She looked swiftly at him, appraising him from a new viewpoint, feeling a strange, new interest in him.

"It would be strange if they didn't," she returned. "Why, it is the only part of the country in which there still remains a touch of romance. You must remember that this is a young country; that its history began at a comparatively late date. England can write of its feudal barons; France of its ancient aristocracy; but America can look back only to the Colonial period—and the West."

"Mebbe you're right," he said, not convinced. "But I expect there ain't a heap of romance out here. Leastways, if there is it manages to keep itself pretty well hid."

She smiled, thinking of the romance that surrounded him—of which, plainly, he was not conscious. To him, romance meant the lights, the crowds, the amusements, the glitter and tinsel of the cities of the East, word of which had come to him through various channels. To her these things were no longer novel,—if they had ever been so—and so for her romance must come from the new, the unusual, the unconventional. The West was all this, therefore romance dwelt here.

"Of course it all seems commonplace to you," she returned; "perhaps even monotonous. For you have lived here long."

He laughed. "I've traveled a heap," he said. "I've been in California, Dakota, Wyoming, Texas, an' Arizona. An' now I'm here. Savin' a man meets different people, this country is pretty much all the same."

"You must have had a great deal of experience," she said. "And you are not very old."

He gravely considered her. "I would say that I am about the average age for this country. You see, folks don't live to get very old out here—unless they're mighty careful."

"And you haven't been careful?"

He smiled gravely. "I expect you wouldn't call it careful. But I'm still livin'."

His words were singularly free from boast.

"That means that you have escaped the dangers," she said. "I have heard that a man's safety in this country depends largely upon his ability to shoot quickly and accurately. I suppose you are accounted a good shot?"

The question was too direct. His eyes narrowed craftily.

"I expect you're thinkin' of that book now ma'am," he said. "There's a heap of men c'n shoot. You might say they're all good shots. I've told you about the men who can't shoot good. They're either mighty careful, or they ain't here any more. It's always one or the other."

"Oh, dear!" she exclaimed, shuddering slightly. "In that case I suppose the hero in my story will have to be a good shot." She laughed. "I shouldn't want him to get half way through the story and then be killed because he was clumsy in handling his weapon. I am beginning to believe that I shall have to make him a 'two-gun' man. I understand they are supposed to be very good shots."

"I've seen them that wasn't," he returned gravely and shortly.

"How did you prove that?" she asked suddenly.

But he was not to be snared. "I didn't say I'd proved it," he stated. "But I've seen it proved."

"How proved?"

"Why," he said, his eyes glinting with amusement, "they ain't here any more, ma'am."

"Oh. Then it doesn't follow that because a man wears two guns he is more likely to survive than is the man who wears only one?"

"I reckon not, ma'am."

"I see that you have the bottoms of your holsters tied down," she said, looking at them. "Why have you done that?"

"Well," he declared, drawling his words a little, "I've always found that there ain't any use of takin' chances on an accident. You mightn't live to tell about it. An' havin' the bottoms of your holsters tied down keeps your guns from snaggin'. I've seen men whose guns got snagged when they wanted to use them. They wasn't so active after."

"Then I shall have to make my hero a 'two-gun' man," she said. "That is decided. Now, the next thing to do is to give some attention to his character. I think he ought to be absolutely fearless and honest and incapable of committing a dishonorable deed. Don't you think so?"

While they had talked he had come closer to her and stood beside the shelf rock, one foot resting on it. At her question he suddenly looked down at the foot, shifting it nervously, while a flush started from above the blue scarf at his throat and slowly suffused his face.

"Don't you think so?" she repeated, her eyes meeting his for an instant.

"Why, of course, ma'am," he suddenly answered, the words coming sharply, as though he had only at that instant realized the import of the question.

"Why," said she, aware of his embarrassment, "don't you think there are such men?"

"I expect there are, ma'am," he returned; "but in this country there's a heap of argument could be made about what would be dishonorable. If your two-gun should happen to be a horse thief, or a rustler, I reckon we could get at it right off."

"He shan't be either of those," she declared stoutly. "I don't think he would stoop to such contemptible deeds. In the story he is employed by a ranch owner to kill a rustler whom the owner imagines has been stealing his cattle."

His hands were suddenly behind him, the fingers clenched. His eyes searched her face with an alert, intense gaze. His embarrassment was gone; his expression was saturnine, his eyes narrowed with a slight mockery. And his voice came, cold, deliberate, even.

"I reckon you've got your gun-man true to life, ma'am," he said.

She laughed lightly, amused over the sudden change that she saw and felt in him. "Of course the gun-man doesn't really intend to kill the rustler," she said. "I don't believe I shall have any one killed in the story. The gun-man is merely attracted by the sum of money promised him by the ranch owner, and when he accepts it is only because he is in dire need of work. Don't you think that could be possible?"

"That could happen easy in this country, ma'am," he returned.

She laughed delightedly. "That vindicates my judgment," she declared.

He was regarding her with unwavering eyes. "Is that gun-man goin' to be the hero in your story, ma'am?" he asked quietly.

"Why, of course."

"An' I'm to be him?"

She gave him a defiant glance, though she blushed immediately.

"Why do you ask?" she questioned in reply. "You need have no fear that I will compel my hero to do anything dishonorable."

"I ain't fearin' anything," he returned. "But I'd like to know how you come to think of that. Do writers make them things up out of their own minds, or does someone tell them?"

"Those things generally have their origin in the mind of the writer," she replied.

"Meanin' that you thought of that yourself?" he persisted.

"Of course."

He lifted his foot from the rock and stood looking gravely at her. "In most of the books I have read there's always a villain. I reckon you're goin' to have one?"

"There will be a villain," she returned.

His eyes flashed queerly. "Would you mind tellin' me who you have picked out for your villain?" he continued.

"I don't mind," she said. "It is Leviatt."

He suddenly grinned broadly and held out his right hand to her. "Shake, ma'am," he said. "I reckon if I was writin' a book Leviatt would be the villain."

She rose from the rock and took his outstretched hand, her eyes drooping as they met his. He felt her hand tremble a little, and he looked at it, marveling. She glanced up, saw him looking at her hand, swiftly withdrew it, and turned from him, looking down into the flat at the base of the hill. She started, uttering the sharp command:

"Look!"

Perhaps a hundred yards distant, sitting on his pony in a lounging attitude, was a horseman. While they looked the horseman removed his broad brimmed hat, bowed mockingly, and urged his pony out into the flat. It was Leviatt.

On the slight breeze a laugh floated back to them, short, sharp, mocking.

For a time they stood silent, watching the departing rider. Then Ferguson's lips wreathed into a feline smile.

"Kind of dramatic, him ridin' up that-a-way," he said. "Don't you think puttin' him in the book will spoil it, ma'am?"

CHAPTER XIII

"DO YOU SMOKE?"

Leviatt rode down through the gully where Miss Radford had first caught sight of Ferguson when he had entered the flat. He disappeared in this and five minutes later came out upon a ridge above it. The distance was too great to observe whether he turned to look back. But just before he disappeared finally they saw him sweep his hat from his head. It was a derisive motion, and Miss Radford colored and shot a furtive glance at Ferguson.

The latter stood loosely beside her, his hat brim pulled well down over his forehead. As she looked she saw his eyes narrow and his lips curve ironically.

"What do you suppose he thought?" she questioned, her eyes drooping away from his.

"Him?" Ferguson laughed. "I expect you could see from his actions that he wasn't a heap tickled." Some thought was moving him mightily. He chuckled gleefully. "Now if you could only put what he was thinkin' into your book, ma'am, it sure would make interestin' readin'."

"But he saw you holding my hand!" she declared, aware of the uselessness of telling him this, but unable to repress her indignation over the thought that Leviatt had seen.

"Why, I expect he did, ma'am!" he returned, trying hard to keep the pleasure out of his voice. "You see, he must have been lookin' right at us. But there ain't nothin' to be flustered over. I reckon that some day, if he's around, he'll see me holdin' your hand again."

The red in her cheeks deepened. "Why, how conceited you are!" she said, trying to be very severe, but only succeeding in making him think that her eyes were prettier than he had thought.

"I don't think I am conceited, ma'am," he returned, smiling. "I've liked you right well since the beginning. I don't think it's conceit to tell a lady that you're thinkin' of holdin' her hand."

She was looking straight at him, trying to be very defiant. "And so you have liked me?" she taunted. "I am considering whether to tell you that I was not thinking of you as a possible admirer."

His eyes flashed. "I don't think you mean that, ma'am," he said. "You ain't treated me like you treated some others."

"Some others?" she questioned, not comprehending.

He laughed. "Them other Two Diamond men that took a shine to you. I've heard that you talked right sassy to them. But you ain't never been sassy to me. Leastways, you ain't never told me to 'evaporate'."

She was suddenly convulsed. "They have told you that?" she questioned. And then not waiting for an answer she continued more soberly: "And so you thought that in view of what I have said to those men you had been treated comparatively civilly. I am afraid I have underestimated you. Hereafter I shall talk less intimately to you."

"I wouldn't do that, ma'am," he pleaded. "You don't need to be afraid that I'll be too fresh."

"Oh, dear!" she exclaimed, with a pretense of delight. "It will be very nice to know that I can talk to you without fear of your placing a false construction on my words. But I am not afraid of you."

He stepped back from the rock, hitching at his cartridge belt. "I'm goin' over to the Two Diamond now, ma'am," he said. "And since you've said you ain't afraid of me, I'm askin' you if you won't go ridin' with me tomorrow. There's a right pretty stretch of country about fifteen miles up the crick that you'd be tickled over."

Should she tell him that she had explored all of the country within thirty miles? The words trembled on her lips but remained unspoken.

"Why, I don't know," she objected. "Do you think it is quite safe?"

He smiled and stepped away from her, looking back over his shoulder. "Thank you, ma'am," he said. "I'll ride over for you some time in the mornin'." He continued down the hill, loose stones rattling ahead of him. She looked after him, radiant.

"But I didn't say I would go," she called. And then, receiving no answer to this, she waited until he had swung into the saddle and was waving a farewell to her.

"Don't come before ten o'clock!" she advised.

She saw him smile and then she returned to her manuscript.

When the Sun-Gods kissed the crest of the hill and bathed her in the rich rose colors that came straight down to the hill through the rift in the mountains, she rose and gathered up her papers. She had not written another line.

It was late in the afternoon when Leviatt rode up to the door of Stafford's office and dismounted. He took plenty of time walking the short distance that lay between him and the door, and growled a savage reply to a loafing puncher, who asked him a question. Once in the office he dropped glumly into a chair, his eyes glittering vengefully as his gaze rested on Stafford, who sat at his desk, engaged in his accounts. Through the open window Stafford had seen the range boss coming and therefore when the latter had entered he had not looked up.

Presently he finished his work and drew back from the desk. Then he took up a pipe, filled it with tobacco, lighted it, and puffed with satisfaction.

"Nothin's happened?" he questioned, glancing at his range boss.

Leviatt's reply was short. "No. Dropped down to see how things was runnin'."

"Things is quiet," returned Stafford. "There ain't been any cattle missed for a long time. I reckon the new stray-man is doin' some good."

Leviatt's eyes glowed. "If you call gassin' with Mary Radford doin' good, why then, he's doin' it!" he snapped.

"I ain't heard that he's doin' that," returned Stafford.

"I'm tellin' you about it now," said Leviatt. "I seen him to-day; him an' her holdin' hands on top of a hill in Bear Flat." He sneered. "He's a better ladies' man than a gunfighter. I reckon we made a mistake in pickin' him up."

Stafford smiled indulgently. "He's cert'nly a good looker," he said. "I reckon some girls would take a shine to him. But I ain't questionin' his shootin'. I've been in this country a right smart while an' I ain't never seen another man that could bore a can six times while it's in the air."

Leviatt's lips drooped. "He could do that an' not have nerve enough to shoot a coyote. Him not clashin' with Ben Radford proves he ain't got nerve."

Stafford smiled. The story of how the stray-man had closed Leviatt's mouth was still fresh in his memory. He was wondering whether Leviatt knew that he had heard about the incident.

"Suppose you try him?" he suggested. "That'd be as good a way as any to find out if he's got nerve."

Leviatt's face bloated poisonously, but he made no answer. Apparently unaware that he had touched a tender spot Stafford continued.

"Mebbe his game is to get in with the girl, figgerin' that he'll be more liable that way to get a chancst at Ben Radford. But whatever his game is, I ain't interferin'. He's got a season contract an' I ain't breakin' my word with the cuss. I ain't takin' no chances with him."

Leviatt rose abruptly, his face swelling with an anger that he was trying hard to suppress. "He'd better not go to foolin' with Mary Radford, damn him!" he snapped.

"I reckon that wind is blowin' in two directions," grinned Stafford. "When I see him I'll tell him—" A clatter of hoofs reached the ears of the two men, and Stafford turned to the window. "Here's the stray-man now," he said gravely.

Both men were silent when Ferguson reached the door. He stood just inside, looking at Stafford and Leviatt with cold, alert eyes. He nodded shortly to Stafford, not removing his gaze from the range boss. The latter deliberately turned his back and looked out of the window.

There was insolence in the movement, but apparently it had no effect upon the stray-man, beyond bringing a queer twitch into the corners of his mouth. He smiled at Stafford.

"Anything new?" questioned the latter, as he had questioned Leviatt.

"Nothin' doin'," returned Ferguson.

Leviatt now turned from the window. He spoke to Stafford, sneering. "Ben Radford's quite a piece away from where he's hangin' out," he said. He again turned to the window.

Ferguson's lips smiled, but his eyes narrowed. Stafford stiffened in his chair. He watched the stray-man's hands furtively, fearing the outcome of this meeting. But Ferguson's hands were nowhere near his guns. They were folded over his chest—lightly—the fingers of his right hand caressing his chin.

"You ridin' up the crick to-day?" he questioned of Leviatt. His tone was mild, yet there was a peculiar quality in it that hinted at hardness.

"No," answered Leviatt, without turning.

Ferguson began rolling a cigarette. When he had done this he lighted it and puffed slowly. "Well, now," he said, "that's mighty peculiar. I'd swore that I saw you over in Bear Flat."

Leviatt turned. "You've been pickin' posies too long with Mary Radford," he sneered.

Ferguson smiled. "Mebbe I have," he returned. "There's them that she'll let pick posies with her, an' them that she won't."

Leviatt's face crimsoned with anger. "I reckon if you hadn't been monkeyin' around too much with the girl, you'd have run across that dead Two Diamond cow an' the dogie that she left," he sneered.

Ferguson's lips straightened. "How far off was you standin' when that cow died?" he drawled.

A curse writhed through Leviatt's lips. "Why, you damned—"

"Don't!" warned Ferguson. He coolly stepped toward Leviatt, holding by the thongs the leather tobacco pouch from which he had obtained the tobacco to make his cigarette. When he had approached close to the range boss he held the pouch up before his eyes.

"I reckon you'd better have a smoke," he said quietly; "they say it's good for the nerves." He took a long pull at the cigarette. "It's pretty fair tobacco," he continued. "I found it about ten miles up the crick, on a ridge above a dry arroyo. I reckon it's your'n. It's got your initials on it."

The eyes of the two men met in a silent battle. Leviatt's were the first to waver. Then he reached out and took the pouch. "It's mine," he said shortly. Again he looked straight at Ferguson, his eyes carrying a silent message.

"You see anything else?" he questioned.

Ferguson smiled. "I ain't sayin' anything about anything else," he returned.

Thus, unsuspectingly, did Stafford watch and listen while these two men arranged to carry on their war man to man, neither asking any favor from the man who, with a word, might have settled it. With his reply that he wasn't "sayin' anything about anything else," Ferguson had told Leviatt that he had no intention of telling his suspicions to any man. Nor from this moment would Leviatt dare whisper a derogatory word into the manager's ear concerning Ferguson.

CHAPTER XIV

ON THE EDGE OF THE PLATEAU

Now that Ferguson was satisfied beyond doubt that Leviatt had been concealed in the thicket above the bed of the arroyo where he had come upon the dead Two Diamond cow, there remained but one disturbing thought: who was the man he had seen riding along the ridge away from the arroyo? Until he discovered the identity of the rider he must remain absolutely in the dark concerning Leviatt's motive in concealing the name of this other actor in the incident. He was positive that Leviatt knew the rider, but he was equally positive that Leviatt would keep this knowledge to himself.

But on this morning he was not much disturbed over the mystery. Other things were troubling him. Would Miss Radford go riding with him? Would she change her mind over night?

As he rode he consulted his silver timepiece. She had told him not to come before ten. The hands of his watch pointed to ten thirty when he entered the flat, and it was near eleven when he rode up to the cabin door—to find Miss Radford—arrayed in riding skirt, dainty boots, gauntleted gloves, blouse, and soft felt hat—awaiting him at the door.

"You're late," she said, smiling as she came out upon the porch.

If he had been less wise he might have told her that she had told him not to come until after ten and that he had noticed that she had been waiting for him in spite of her apparent reluctance of yesterday. But he steered carefully away from this pitfall. He dismounted and threw the bridle rein over Mustard's head, coming around beside the porch.

"I wasn't thinkin' to hurry you, ma'am," he said. "But I reckon we'll go now. It's cert'nly a fine day for ridin'." He stood silent for a moment, looking about him. Then he flushed. "Why, I'm gettin' right box-headed, ma'am," he declared. "Here I am standin' an' makin' you sick with my palaver, an' your horse waitin' to be caught up."

He stepped quickly to Mustard's side and uncoiled his rope. She stood on the porch, watching him as he proceeded to the corral, caught the pony, and flung a bridle on it. Then he led the animal to the porch and cinched the saddle carefully. Throwing the reins over the pommel of the saddle, he stood at the animal's head, waiting.

She came to the edge of the porch, placed a slender, booted foot into the ox-bow stirrup, and swung gracefully up. In an instant he had vaulted into his own saddle, and together they rode out upon the gray-white floor of the flat.

They rode two miles, keeping near the fringe of cottonwoods, and presently mounted a long slope. Half an hour later Miss Radford looked back and saw the flat spread out behind, silent, vast, deserted, slumbering in the swimming white sunlight. A little later she looked again, and the flat was no longer there, for they had reached the crest of the slope and their trail had wound them round to a broad level, from which began another slope, several miles distant.

They had ridden for more than two hours, talking very little, when they reached the crest of the last rise and saw, spreading before them, a level many miles wide, stretching away in three directions. It was a grass plateau, but the grass was dry and drooping and rustled under the ponies' hoofs. There were no trees, but a post oak thicket skirted the southern edge, and it was toward this that he urged his pony. She followed, smiling to think that he was deceiving himself in believing that she had not yet explored this place.

They came close to the thicket, and he swung off his horse and stood at her stirrup.

"I was wantin' you to see the country from here," he said, as he helped her down. She watched him while he picketed the horses, so that they might not stray. Then they went together to the edge of the thicket, seating themselves in a welcome shade.

At their feet the plateau dropped sheer, as though cut with a knife, and a little way out from the base lay a narrow ribbon of water that flowed slowly in its rocky bed, winding around the base of a small hill, spreading over a shallow bottom, and disappearing between the buttes farther down.

Everything beneath them was distinguishable, though distant. Knobs rose here; there a flat spread. Mountains frowned in the distance, but so far away that they seemed like papier-mache shapes towering in a sea of blue. Like a map the country seemed as Miss Radford and Ferguson looked down upon it, yet a big map, over which one might wonder; more vast, more nearly perfect, richer in detail than any that could be evolved from the talents of man.

Ridges, valleys, gullies, hills, knobs, and draws were all laid out in a vast basin. Miss Radford's gaze swept down into a section of flat near the river.

"Why, there are some cattle down there!" she exclaimed.

"Sure," he returned; "they're Two Diamond. Way off there behind that ridge is where the wagon is." He pointed to a long range of flat hills that stretched several miles. "The boys that are workin' on the other side of that ridge can't see them cattle like we can. Looks plum re-diculous."

"There are no men with those cattle down there," she said, pointing to those below in the flat.

"No," he returned quietly; "they're all off on the other side of the ridge."

She smiled demurely at him. "Then we won't be interrupted—as we were yesterday," she said.

Did she know that this was why he had selected this spot for the end of the ride? He looked quickly at her, but answered slowly.

"They couldn't see us," he said. "If we was out in the open we'd be right on the skyline. Then anyone could see us. But we've got this thicket behind us, an' I reckon from down there we'd be pretty near invisible."

He turned around, clasping his hands about one knee and looking squarely at her. "I expect you done a heap with your book yesterday—after I went away?"

Her cheeks colored a little under his straight gaze.

"I didn't stay there long," she equivocated. "But I got some very good ideas, and I am glad that I didn't write much. I should have had to destroy it, because I have decided upon a different beginning. Ben made the trip to Dry Bottom yesterday, and last night he told something that had happened there that has given me some very good material for a beginning."

"That's awful interestin'," he observed. "So now you'll be able to start your book with somethin' that really happened?"

"Real and original," she returned, with a quick glance at him. "Ben told me that about a month ago some men had a shooting match in Dry Bottom. They used a can for a target, and one man kept it in the air until he put six bullet holes through it. Ben says he is pretty handy with his weapons, but he could never do that. He insists that few men can, and he is inclined to think that the man who did do it must have been a gunfighter. I suppose you have never tried it?"

Over his lips while she had been speaking had crept the slight mocking smile which always told better than words of the cold cynicism that moved him at times. Did she know anything? Did she suspect him? The smile masked an interest that illumined his eyes very slightly as he looked at her.

"I expect that is plum slick shootin'," he returned slowly. "But some men can do it. I've knowed them. But I ain't heard that it's been done lately in this here country. I reckon Ben told you somethin' of how this man looked?"

He had succeeded in putting the question very casually, and she had not caught the note of deep interest in his voice.

"Why it's very odd," she said, looking him over carefully; "from Ben's description I should assume that the man looked very like you!"

If her reply had startled him he gave little evidence of it. He sat perfectly quiet, gazing with steady eyes out over the big basin. For a time she sat silent also, her gaze following his. Then she turned.

"That would be odd, wouldn't it?" she said.

"What would?" he answered, not looking at her.

"Why, if you *were* the man who had done that shooting! It would follow out the idea of my plot perfectly. For in my story the hero is hired to shoot a supposed rustler, and of course he would have to be a good shot. And since Ben has told me the story of the shooting match I have decided that the hero in my story shall be tested in that manner before being employed to shoot the rustler. Then he comes to the supposed rustler's cabin and meets the heroine, in much the same manner that you came. Now if it should turn out that you were the man who did the shooting in Dry Bottom my story up to this point would be very nearly real. And that would be fine!"

She had allowed a little enthusiasm to creep into her voice, and he looked up at her quickly, a queer expression in his eyes.

"You goin' to have your 'two-gun' man bit by a rattler?" he questioned.

"Well, I don't know about that. It would make very little difference. But I should be delighted to find that you were the man who did the shooting over at Dry Bottom. Say that you are!"

Even now he could not tell whether there was subtlety in her voice The old doubt rose again in his mind. Was she really serious in saying that she intended putting all this in her story, or was this a ruse, concealing an ulterior purpose? Suppose she and her brother suspected him of being the man who had participated in the shooting match in Dry Bottom? Suppose the brother, or she, had invented this tale about the book to draw him out? He was moved to an inward humor, amused to think that either of them should imagine him shallow enough to be caught thus.

But what if they did catch him? Would they gain by it? They could gain nothing, but the knowledge would serve to put them on their guard. But if she did suspect him, what use was there in evasion or denial? He smiled whimsically.

"I reckon your story is goin' to be real up to this point," he returned. "A while back I did shoot at a can in Dry Bottom."

She gave an exclamation of delight. "Now, isn't that marvelous? No one shall be able to say that my beginning will be strictly fiction." She leaned closer to him, her eyes alight with eagerness. "Now please don't say that you are the man who shot the can five times," she pleaded. "I shouldn't want my hero to be beaten at anything he undertook. But I know that you were not beaten. Were you?"

He smiled gravely. "I reckon I wasn't beat," he returned.

She sat back and surveyed him with satisfaction.

"I knew it," she stated, as though in her mind there had never existed any doubt of the fact. "Now," she said, plainly pleased over the result of her questioning, "I shall be able to proceed, entirely confident that my hero will be able to give a good account of himself in any situation."

Her eyes baffled him. He gave up watching her and turned to look at the world beneath him. He would have given much to know her thoughts. She had said that from her brother's description of the man who had won the shooting match at Dry Bottom she would assume that that man had looked very like him. Did her brother hold this opinion also?

Ferguson cared very little if he did. He was accustomed to danger, and he had gone into this business with his eyes open. And if Ben did know—Unconsciously his lips straightened and his chin went forward slightly, giving his face an expression of hardness that made him look ten years older. Watching him, the girl drew a slow, full breath. It was a side of his character with which she was as yet unacquainted, and she marveled over it, comparing it to the side she already knew—the side that he had shown her—quiet, thoughtful, subtle. And now at a glance she saw him as men knew him—unyielding, unafraid, indomitable.

Yet there was much in this sudden revelation of character to admire. She liked a man whom other men respected for the very traits that his expression had revealed. No man would be likely to adopt an air of superiority toward him; none would attempt to trifle with him. She felt that she ought not to trifle, but moved by some unaccountable impulse, she laughed.

He turned his head at the laugh and looked quizzically at her.

"I hope you were not thinking of killing some one?" she taunted.

His right hand slowly clenched. Something metallic suddenly glinted his eyes, to be succeeded instantly by a slight mockery. "You afraid some one's goin' to be killed?" he inquired slowly.

"Well—no," she returned, startled by the question. "But you looked so—so determined that I—I thought—"

He suddenly seized her arm and drew her around so that she faced the little stretch of plain near the ridge about which they had been speaking previously. His lips were in straight lines again, his eyes gleaming interestedly.

"You see that man down there among them cattle?" he questioned.

Following his gaze, she saw a man among perhaps a dozen cattle. At the moment she looked the man had swung a rope, and she saw the loop fall true over the head of a cow the man had selected, saw the pony pivot and drag the cow prone. Then the man dismounted, ran swiftly to the side of the fallen cow, and busied himself about her hind legs.

"What is he doing?" she asked, a sudden excitement shining in her eyes.

"He's hog-tieing her now," returned Ferguson.

She knew what that meant. She had seen Ben throw cattle in this manner when he was branding them. "Hog-tieing" meant binding their hind legs with a short piece of rope to prevent struggling while the brand was being applied.

Apparently this was what the man was preparing to do. Smoke from a nearby fire curled lazily upward, and about this fire the man now worked—evidently turning some branding irons. He gave some little time to this, and while Miss Radford watched she heard Ferguson's voice again.

"I reckon we're goin' to see some fun pretty soon," he said quietly.

"Why?" she inquired quickly.

He smiled. "Do you see that man ridin' through that break on the ridge?" he asked, pointing the place out to her. She nodded, puzzled by his manner. He continued dryly.

"Well, if that man that's comin' through the break is what he ought to be he'll be shootin' pretty soon."

"Why?" she gasped, catching at his sleeve, "why should he shoot?"

He laughed again—grimly. "Well," he returned, "if a puncher ketches a rustler with the goods on he's got a heap of right to do some shootin'."

She shuddered. "And do you think that man among the cattle is a rustler?" she asked.

"Wait," he advised, peering intently toward the ridge. "Why," he continued presently, "there's another man ridin' this way. An' he's hidin' from the other—keepin' in the gullies an' the draws so's the first man can't see him if he looks back." He laughed softly. "It's plum re-diculous. Here we are, able to see all that's goin' on down there an' not able to take a hand in it. An' there's them three goin' ahead with what they're thinkin' about, not knowin' that we're watchin' them, an' two of them not knowin' that the third man is watchin'. I'd call that plum re-diculous."

The first man was still riding through the break in the ridge, coming boldly, apparently unconscious of the presence of the man among the cattle, who was well concealed from the first man's eyes by a rocky promontory at the corner of the break. The third man was not over an eighth of a mile behind the first man, and riding slowly and carefully. At the rate the first man was riding not five minutes would elapse before he would come out into the plain full upon the point where the man among the cattle was working at his fire.

Ferguson and Miss Radford watched the scene with interest. Plainly the first man was intruding. Or if not, he was the rustler's confederate and the third man was spying upon him. Miss Radford and Ferguson were to discover the key to the situation presently.

"Do you think that man among the cattle is a rustler?" questioned Miss Radford. In her excitement she had pressed very close to Ferguson and was clutching his arm very tightly.

"I reckon he is," returned Ferguson. "I ain't rememberin' that any ranch has cows that run the range unbranded; especially when the cow has got a calf, unless that cow is a maverick, an' that ain't likely, since she's runnin' with the Two Diamond bunch."

He leaned forward, for the man had left the fire and was running toward the fallen cow. Once at her side the man bent over her, pressing the hot irons against the bottoms of her hoofs. A thin wreath of smoke curled upward; the cow struggled.

Ferguson looked at Miss Radford. "Burnt her hoofs," he said shortly, "so she can't follow when he runs her calf off."

"The brute!" declared Miss Radford, her face paling with anger.

The man was fumbling with the rope that bound the cow's legs, when the first man rode around the edge of the break and came full upon him. From the distance at which Miss Radford and Ferguson watched they could not see the expression of either man's face, but they saw the rustler's right hand move downward; saw his pistol glitter in the sunlight.

But the pistol was not raised. The first man's pistol had appeared just a fraction of a second sooner, and they saw that it was poised, menacing the rustler.

For an instant the two men were motionless. Ferguson felt the grasp on his arm tighten, and he turned his head to see Miss Radford's face, pale and drawn; her eyes lifted to his with a slow, dawning horror in them.

"Oh!" she exclaimed. "They are going to shoot!" She withdrew her hand from Ferguson's arm and held it, with the other, to her ears, cringing away from the edge of the cliff. She waited, breathless, for—it seemed to her—the space of several minutes, her head turned from the men, her eyes closed for fear that she might, in the dread of the moment, look toward the plain. She kept telling herself that she would not turn, but presently, in spite of her determination, the suspense was too great, and she turned quickly and fearfully, expecting to see at least one riderless horse. That would have been horrible enough.

To her surprise both men still kept the positions that they had held when she had turned away. The newcomer's revolver still menaced the rustler. She looked up into Ferguson's face, to see a grim smile on it, to see his eyes, chilled and narrowed, fixed steadily upon the two horsemen.

"Oh!" she said, "is it over?"

Ferguson heard the question, and smiled mirthlessly without turning his head.

"I reckon it ain't over—yet," he returned. "But I expect it'll be over pretty soon, if that guy that's got his gun on the rustler don't get a move on right quick. That other guy is comin' around the corner of that break, an' if he's the rustler's friend that man with the gun will get his pretty rapid." His voice raised a trifle, a slightly anxious note in it.

"Why don't the damn fool turn around? He could see that last man now if he did. Now, what do you think of that?" Ferguson's voice was sharp and tense, and, in spite of herself, Miss Radford's gaze shifted again to the plains below her. Fascinated, her fear succumbing to the intense interest of the moment, she followed the movements of the trio.

From around the corner of the break the third man had ridden. He was not over a hundred feet from the man who had caught the rustler and he was walking his horse now. The watchers on the edge of the plateau could see that he had taken in the situation and was stealing upon the captor, who sat in his saddle, his back to the advancing rider.

Drawing a little closer, the third man stealthily dropped from his pony and crept forward. The significance of this movement dawned upon Miss Radford in a flash, and she again seized Ferguson's arm, tugging at it fiercely.

"Why, he's going to kill that man!" she cried. "Can't you do something? For mercy's sake do! Shout, or shoot off your pistol—do something to warn him!"

Ferguson flashed a swift glance at her, and she saw that his face wore a queer pallor. His expression had grown grimmer, but he smiled—a little sadly, she thought.

"It ain't a bit of use tryin' to do anything," he returned, his gaze again on the men. "We're two miles from them men an' a thousand feet above them. There ain't any pistol report goin' to stop what's goin' on down there. All we can do is to watch. Mebbe we can recognize one of them . . . Shucks!"

The exclamation was called from him by a sudden movement on the part of the captor. The third man must have made a noise, for the captor turned sharply. At the instant he did so the rustler's pistol flashed in the sunlight.

The watchers on the plateau did not hear the report at once, and when they did it came to them only faintly—a slight sound which was barely distinguishable. But they saw a sudden spurt of flame and smoke. The captor reeled drunkenly in his saddle, caught blindly at the pommel, and then slid slowly down into the grass of the plains.

Ferguson drew a deep breath and, turning, looked sharply at Miss Radford. She had covered her face with her hands and was swaying dizzily. He was up from the rock in a flash and was supporting her, leading her away from the edge of the plateau. She went unresisting, her slender figure shuddering spasmodically, her hands still covering her face.

"Oh!" she exclaimed, as the horror of the scene rose in her mind. "The brutes! The brutes!"

Feeling that if he kept quiet she would recover from the shock of the incident sooner, Ferguson said nothing in reply to her outbreaks as he led her toward the ponies. For a moment after reaching them she leaned against her animal's shoulder, her face concealed from Ferguson by the pony's mane. Then he was at her side, speaking firmly.

"You must get away from here," he said, "I ought to have got you away before—before that happened."

She looked up, showing him a pair of wide, dry eyes, in which there was still a trace of horror. An expression of grave self-accusation shone in his.

"You were not to blame," she said dully. "You may have anticipated a meeting of those men, but you could not have foreseen the end. Oh!" She shuddered again. "To think of seeing a man deliberately murdered!"

"That's just what it was," he returned quietly; "just plain murder. They had him between them. He didn't have a chance. He was bound to get it from one or the other. Looks like they trapped him; run him down there on purpose." He held her stirrup.

"I reckon you've seen enough, ma'am," he added. "You'd better hop right on your horse an' get back to Bear Flat."

She shivered and raised her head, looking at him—a flash of fear in her eyes. "You are going down there!" she cried, her eyes dilating.

He laughed grimly. "I cert'nly am, ma'am," he returned. "You'd better go right off. I'm ridin' down there to see how bad that man is hit."

She started toward him, protesting. "Why, they will kill you, too!" she declared.

He laughed again, with a sudden grim humor. "There ain't any danger," he returned. "They've sloped."

Involuntarily she looked down. Far out on the plains, through the break in the ridge of hills, she could see two horsemen racing away.

"The cowards!" she cried, her voice shaking with anger. "To shoot a man in cold blood and then run!" She looked at Ferguson, her figure stiffening with decision.

"If you go down there I am going, too!" she declared. "He might need some help," she added, seeing the objection in his eyes, "and if he does I may be able to give it to him. You know," she continued, smiling wanly, "I have had some experience with sick people."

He said nothing more, but silently assisted her into the saddle and swung into his own. They urged the animals to a rapid pace, she following him eagerly.

It was a rough trail, leading through many gullies, around miniature hills, into bottoms where huge boulders and treacherous sand barred the way, along the face of dizzy cliffs, and through lava beds where the footing was uncertain and dangerous. But in an hour they were on the plains and riding toward the break in the ridge of hills, where the shooting had been done.

The man's pony had moved off a little and was grazing unconcernedly when they arrived. A brown heap in the grass told where the man lay, and presently Ferguson was down beside him, one of his limp wrists between his fingers. He stood up after a moment, to confront Miss Radford, who had fallen behind during the last few minutes of the ride. Ferguson's face was grave, and there was a light in his eyes that thrilled her for a moment as she looked at him.

"He ain't dead, ma'am," he said as he assisted her down from her pony. "The bullet got him in the shoulder."

She caught a queer note in his voice—something approaching appeal. She looked swiftly at him, suspicious. "Do you know him?" she asked.

"I reckon I do, ma'am," he returned. "It's Rope Jones. Once he stood by me when he thought I needed a friend. If there's any chance I'm goin' to get him to your cabin—where you can take care of him till he gets over this—if he ever does."

She realized now how this tragedy had shocked her. She reeled and the world swam dizzily before her. Again she saw Ferguson dart forward, but she steadied herself and smiled reassuringly.

"It is merely the thought that I must now put my little knowledge to a severe test," she said. "It rather frightened me. I don't know whether anything can be done."

She succeeded in forcing herself to calmness and gave orders rapidly.

"Get something under his head," she commanded. "No, that will be too high," she added, as she saw Ferguson start to unbuckle the saddle cinch on his pony. "Raise his head only a very little. That round thing that you have fastened to your saddle (the slicker) would do very well. There. Now get some water!"

She was down beside the wounded man in another instant, cutting away a section of the shirt near the shoulder, with a knife that she had borrowed from Ferguson. The wound had not bled much and was lower than Ferguson had thought. But she gave it what care she could, and when Ferguson arrived with water—from the river, a mile away—she dressed the wound and applied water to Rope's forehead.

Soon she saw that her efforts were to be of little avail. Rope lay pitifully slack and unresponsive. At the end of an hour's work Ferguson bent over her with a question on his lips.

"Do you reckon he'll come around, ma'am?"

She shook her head negatively. "The bullet has lodged somewhere—possibly in the lung," she returned. "It entered just above the heart, and he has bled much—internally. He may never regain consciousness."

Ferguson's face paled with a sudden anger. "In that case, ma'am, we'll never know who shot him," he said slowly. "An' I'm wantin' to know that. Couldn't you fetch him to, ma'am—just long enough so's I could ask him?"

She looked up with a slow glance. "I can try," she said. "Is there any more whiskey in your flask?"

He produced the flask, and they both bent over Rope, forcing a generous portion of the liquor down his throat. Then, alternately bathing the wound and his forehead, they watched. They were rewarded presently by a faint flicker of the eyelids and a slow flow of color in the pale cheeks. Then after a little the eyes opened.

In an instant Ferguson's lips were close to Rope's ear. "Who shot you, Rope, old man?" he asked eagerly. "You don't need to be afraid to tell me, it's Ferguson."

The wounded man's eyes were glazed with a dull incomprehension. But slowly, as though at last he was faintly conscious of the significance of the question, his eyes glinted with the steady light of returning reason. Suddenly he smiled, his lips opening slightly. Both watchers leaned tensely forward to catch the low words.

"Ferguson told me to look out," he mumbled. "He told me to be careful that they didn't get me between them. But I wasn't thinkin' it would happen just that way." And now his eyes opened scornfully and he struggled and lifted himself upon one arm, gazing at some imaginary object.

"Why," he said slowly and distinctly, his voice cold and metallic, "you're a hell of a range boss! Why you—!" he broke off suddenly, his eyes fixed full upon Miss Radford. "Why, it's a woman! An' I thought—Why, ma'am," he went on, apologetically, "I didn't know you was there! . . . But you ain't goin' to run off no calf while I'm lookin' at you. Shucks! Won't the Ol' Man be some surprised to know that Tucson an'—"

He shuddered spasmodically and sat erect with a great effort.

"You've got me, damn you!" he sneered. "But you won't never get anyone—"

He swung his right hand over his head, as though the hand held a pistol. But the arm suddenly dropped, he shuddered again, and sank slowly back—his eyes wide and staring, but unseeing.

Ferguson looked sharply at Miss Radford, who was suddenly bending over the prostrate man, her head on his breast. She arose after a little, tears starting to her eyes.

"He has gone," she said slowly.

CHAPTER XV

A FREE HAND

It was near midnight when Ferguson rode in to the Two Diamond ranchhouse leading Rope's pony. He carefully unsaddled the two animals and let them into the corral, taking great pains to make little noise. Rope's saddle—a peculiar one with a high pommel bearing a silver plate upon which the puncher's name was engraved—he placed conspicuously near the door of the bunkhouse. His own he carefully suspended from its accustomed hook in the lean-to. Then, still carefully, he made his way inside the bunkhouse and sought his bunk.

At dawn he heard voices outside and he arose and went to the door. Several of the men were gathered about the step talking. For an instant Ferguson stood, his eyes roving over the group. Tucson was not there. He went back into the bunkhouse and walked casually about, taking swift glances at the bunks where the men still slept. Then he returned to the door, satisfied that Tucson had not come in.

When he reached the door again he found that the men of the group had discovered the saddle. One of them was saying something about it. "That ain't just the way I take care of my saddle," he was telling the others; "leavin' her out nights."

"I never knowed Rope to be that careless before," said another.

Ferguson returned to the bunkhouse and ate breakfast. After the meal was finished he went out, caught up Mustard, swung into the saddle, and rode down to the ranchhouse door. He found Stafford in the office. The latter greeted the stray-man with a smile.

"Somethin' doin'?" he questioned.

"You might call it that," returned Ferguson. He went inside and seated himself near Stafford's desk.

"I've come in to tell you that I saw some rustlers workin' on the herd yesterday," he said.

Stafford sat suddenly erect, his eyes lighting interrogatively.

"It wasn't Ben Radford," continued Ferguson, answering the look. "You'd be surprised if I told you. But I ain't tellin'—now. I'm waitin' to see if someone else does. But I'm tellin' you this: They got Rope Jones."

Stafford's face reddened with anger. "They got Rope, you say?" he demanded. "Why, where—damn them!"

"Back of the ridge about fifteen miles up the crick," returned Ferguson. "I was ridin' along the edge of the plateau an' I saw a man down there shoot another. I got down as soon as I could an' found Rope. There wasn't nothin' I could do. So I planted him where I found him an' brought his horse back. There was two rustlers there. But only one done the shootin'. I got the name of one."

Stafford cursed. "I'm wantin' to know who it was!" he demanded. "I'll make him—why, damn him, I'll—"

"You're carryin' on awful," observed Ferguson dryly. "But you ain't doin' any good." He leaned closer to Stafford. "I'm quittin' my job right now," he said.

Stafford leaned back in his chair, surprised into silence. For an instant he glared at the stray-man, and then his lips curled scornfully.

"So you're quittin'," he sneered; "scared plum out because you seen a man put out of business! I reckon Leviatt wasn't far wrong when he said—"

"I wouldn't say a lot," interrupted Ferguson coldly. "I ain't admittin' that I'm any scared. An' I ain't carin' a heap because Leviatt's been gassin' to you. But I'm quittin' the job you give me. Ben Radford ain't the man who's been rustlin' your cattle. It's someone else. I'm askin' you to hire me to find out whoever it is. I'm wantin' a free hand. I don't want anyone askin' me any questions. I don't want anyone orderin' me around. But if you want the men who are rustlin' your cattle, I'm offerin' to do the job. Do I get it?"

"You're keepin' right on—workin' for the Two Diamond," returned Stafford. "But I'd like to get hold of the man who got Rope."

Ferguson smiled grimly. "That man'll be gittin' his some day," he declared, rising. "I'm keepin' him for myself. Mebbe I won't shoot him. I reckon Rope'd be some tickled if he'd know that the man who shot him could get a chance to think it over while some man was stringin' him up. You ain't sayin' anything about anything."

He turned and went out. Five minutes later Stafford saw him riding slowly toward the river.

As the days went a mysterious word began to be spoken wherever men congregated. No man knew whence the word had come, but it was whispered that Rope Jones would be seen no more. His pony joined the remuda; his saddle and other personal effects became prizes for which the men of the outfit cast lots. Inquiries were made concerning the puncher by friends who persisted in being inquisitive, but nothing resulted. In time the word "rustler" became associated with his name, and "caught with the goods" grew to be a phrase that told eloquently of the manner of his death. Later it was whispered that Leviatt and Tucson had come upon Rope behind the ridge, catching him in the act of running off a Two Diamond calf. But as no report had been made to Stafford by either Leviatt or Tucson, the news remained merely rumor.

Ferguson had said nothing more to any man concerning the incident. To do so would have warned Tucson. And neither Ferguson nor Miss Radford could have sworn to the man's guilt. In addition to this, there lingered in Ferguson's mind a desire to play this game in his own way. Telling the men of the outfit what he had seen would make his knowledge common property—and in the absence of proof might cause him to appear ridiculous.

But since the shooting he had little doubt that Leviatt had been Tucson's companion on that day. Rope's scathing words—spoken while Miss Radford had been trying to revive him—. "You're a hell of a range boss," had convinced the stray-man that Leviatt had been one of the assailants. He had wondered much over the emotions of the two when they returned to the spot where the murder had been committed, to find their victim buried and his horse gone. But of one thing he was certain—their surprise over the discovery that the body of their victim had been buried could not have equalled their discomfiture on learning that the latter's pony had been secretly brought to the home ranch, and that among the men of the outfit was one, at least, who knew something of their guilty secret. Ferguson thought this to be the reason that they had not reported the incident to Stafford.

There was now nothing for the stray-man to do but watch. The men who had killed Rope were wary and dangerous, and their next move might be directed at him. But he was not disturbed. One thought brought him a mighty satisfaction. He was no longer employed to fasten upon Ben Radford the stigma of guilt; no longer need he feel oppressed with the guilty consciousness, when in the presence of Mary Radford, that he was, in a measure, a hired spy whose business it was to convict her brother of the crime of rustling. He might now meet the young woman face to face, without experiencing the sensation of guilt that had always affected him.

Beneath his satisfaction lurked a deeper emotion. During the course of his acquaintance with Rope Jones he had developed a sincere affection for the man. The grief in his heart over Rope's death was made more poignant because of the latter's words, just before the final moment, which seemed to have been a plea for vengeance:

"Ferguson told me to look out. He told me to be careful that they didn't get me between them. But I wasn't thinkin' that it would happen just that way."

This had been all that Rope had said about his friend, but it showed that during his last conscious moments he had been thinking of the stray-man. As the days passed the words dwelt continually in Ferguson's mind. Each day that he rode abroad, searching for evidence against the murderers, brought him a day nearer to the vengeance upon which he had determined.

CHAPTER XVI

LEVIATT TAKES A STEP

Miss Radford was sitting on the flat rock on the hill where she had written the first page of her novel. The afternoon sun was coming slantwise over the western mountains, sinking steadily toward the rift out of which came the rose veil that she had watched many times. She had just completed a paragraph in which the villain appears when she became aware of someone standing near. She turned swiftly, with heightened color, to see Leviatt.

His sudden appearance gave her something of a shock, for as he stood there, smiling at her, he answered perfectly the description she had just written. He might have just stepped from one of her pages. But the shock passed, leaving her a little pale, but quite composed—and not a little annoyed. She had found her work interesting; she had become quite absorbed in it. Therefore she failed to appreciate Leviatt's sudden appearance, and with uptilted chin turned from him and pretended an interest in the rim of hills that surrounded the flat.

For an instant Leviatt stood, a frown wrinkling his forehead. Then with a smile he stepped forward and seated himself beside her on the rock. She immediately drew her skirts close to her and shot a displeased glance at him from the corners of her eyes. Then seeing that he still sat there, she moved her belongings a few feet and followed them. He could not doubt the significance of this move, but had he been wise he might have ignored it. A woman's impulses will move her to rebuke a man, but if he will accept without comment he may be reasonably sure of her pity, and pity is a path of promise.

But the range boss neglected his opportunity. He made the mistake of thinking that because he had seen her many times while visiting her brother he might now with propriety assume an air of intimacy toward her.

"I reckon this rock is plenty big enough for both of us," he said amiably.

She measured the distance between them with a calculating eye. "It is," she returned quietly, "if you remain exactly where you are."

He forced a smile. "An' if I don't?" he inquired.

"You may have the rock to yourself," she returned coldly. "I did not ask you to come here."

He chose to ignore this hint, telling her that he had been to the cabin to see Ben and, finding him absent, had ridden through the flat. "I saw you when I was quite a piece away," he concluded, "an' thought mebbe you might be lonesome."

"When I am lonesome I choose my own company," she returned coldly.

"Why, sure," he said, his tone slightly sarcastic; "you cert'nly ought to know who you want to talk to. But you ain't objectin' to me settin' on this hill?" he inquired.

"The hill is not mine," she observed quietly, examining one of the written pages of her novel; "sit here as long as you like."

"Thanks." He drawled the word. Leaning back on one elbow he stretched out as though assured that she would make no further objections to his presence. She ignored him completely and very deliberately arranged her papers and resumed writing.

For a time he lay silent, watching the pencil travel the width of the page—and then back. A mass of completed manuscript lay at her side, the pages covered with carefully written, legible words. She had always taken a pardonable pride in her penmanship. For a while he watched her, puzzled, furtively trying to decipher some of the words that appeared upon the pages. But the distance was too great for him and he finally gave it up and fell to looking at her instead, though determined to solve the wordy mystery that was massed near her.

Finally finding the silence irksome, he dropped an experimental word, speaking casually. "You must have been to school a heap—writin' like you do."

She gave him no answer, being at that moment absorbed in a thought which she was trying to transcribe before it should take wings and be gone forever.

"Writin' comes easy to some people," he persisted.

The thought had been set down; she turned very slightly. "Yes," she said looking steadily at him, "it does. So does impertinence."

He smiled easily. "I ain't aimin' to be impertinent," he returned. "I wouldn't reckon that askin' you what you are writin' would be impertinent. It's too long for a letter."

"It is a novel," she returned shortly.

He smiled, exulting over this partial concession. "I reckon to write a book you must be some special kind of a woman," he observed admiringly.

She was silent. He sat up and leaned toward her, his eyes flashing with a sudden passion.

"If that's it," he said with unmistakable significance, "I don't mind tellin' you that I'm some partial to them special kind."

Her chin rose a little. "I am not concerned over your feelings," she returned without looking at him.

"That kind of a woman would naturally know a heap," he went on, apparently unmindful of the rebuke; "they'd cert'nly know enough to be able to see when a man likes them."

She evidently understood the drift, for her eyes glowed subtly. "It is too bad that you are not a 'special kind of man,' then," she replied.

"Meanin'?" he questioned, his eyes glinting with eagerness.

"Meaning that if you were a 'special kind of man' you would be able to tell when a woman doesn't like you," she said coldly.

"I reckon that I ain't a special kind then," he declared, his face reddening slightly. "Of course, I've seen that you ain't appeared to take much of a shine to me. But I've heard that there's women that can be won if a man keeps at it long enough."

"Some men like to waste their time," she returned quietly.

"I don't call it wastin' time to be talkin' to you," he declared rapidly.

"Our opinions differ," she observed shortly, resting the pencil point on the page that she had been writing.

Her profile was toward him; her cheeks were tinged with color; some stray wisps of hair hung, breeze-blown, over her forehead and temples. She made an attractive picture, sitting there with the soft sunlight about her, a picture whose beauty smote Leviatt's heart with a pang of sudden regret and disappointment. She might have been his, but for the coming of Ferguson. And now, because of the stray-man's wiles, he was losing her.

A sudden rage seized upon him; he leaned forward, his face bloating poisonously. "Mebbe I could name a man who ain't wastin' his time!" he sneered.

She turned suddenly and looked at him, dropping pencil and paper, her eyes flashing with a bitter scorn. "You are one of those sulking cowards who fawn over men and insult defenseless women!" she declared, the words coming slowly and distinctly.

He had realized before she answered that he had erred, and he smiled deprecatingly, the effort contorting his face.

"I wasn't meanin' just that," he said weakly. "I reckon it's a clear field an' no favors." He took a step toward her, his voice growing tense. "I've been comin' down to your cabin a lot, sayin' that I was comin' to see Ben. But I didn't come to see Ben—I wanted to look at you. I reckon you knowed that. A woman can't help but see when a man's in love with her. But you've never give me a chance to tell you. I'm tellin' you now. I want you to marry me. I'm range boss for the Two Diamond an' I've got some stock that's my own, an' money in the bank over in Cimarron. I'll put up a shack a few miles down the river an'—"

"Stop!" commanded Miss Radford imperiously.

Leviatt had been speaking rapidly, absorbed in his subject, assurance shining in his face. But at Miss Radford's command he broke off suddenly and stiffened, surprise widening his eyes.

"You have said enough," she continued; "quite enough. I have never thought of you as a possible admirer. I certainly have done nothing that might lead you to believe I would marry you. I do not even like you—not even respect you. I am not certain that I shall ever marry, but if I do, I certainly shall not marry a man whose every look is an insult."

She turned haughtily and began to gather up her papers. There had been no excitement in her manner; her voice had been steady, even, and tempered with a slight scorn.

For a brief space Leviatt stood, while the full significance of her refusal ate slowly into his consciousness. Whatever hopes he might have had had been swept away in those few short, pithy sentences. His passion checked, the structure erected by his imagination toppled to ruin, his vanity hurt, he stood before her stripped of the veneer that had made him seem, heretofore, nearly the man he professed to be.

In her note book had been written:

"Dave Leviatt... One rather gets the impression that the stoop is a reflection of the man's nature, which seems vindictive and suggests a low cunning. His eyes are small, deep set, and glitter when he talks. But they are steady and cold—almost merciless. One's thoughts go instantly to the tiger. I shall try to create that impression in the reader's mind."

And now as she looked at him she was sure that task would not be difficult. She had now an impression of him that seemed as though it had been seared into her mind. The eyes that she had thought merciless were now glittering malevolently, and she shuddered at the satyric upward curve of his lips as he stepped close to the rock and placed a hand upon the mass of manuscript lying there, that she had previously dropped, to prevent her leaving.

"So you don't love me?" he sneered. "You don't even respect me. Why? Because you've taken a shine to that damned maverick that come here from Dry Bottom—Stafford's new stray-man!"

"That is my business," she returned icily.

"It sure is," he said, the words writhing venomously through his lips. "An' it's my business too. There ain't any damned—"

He had glanced suddenly downward while he had been talking and his gaze rested upon an upturned page of the manuscript that lay beside him on the rock. He broke off speaking and reaching down took up the page, his eyes narrowing with interest. The page he had taken up was one from the first chapter and described in detail the shooting match in Dry Bottom. It was a truthful picture of what had actually happened. She had even used the real names of the characters. Leviatt saw a reference to the "Silver Dollar" saloon, to the loungers, to the stranger who had ridden up and who sat on his pony near the hitching rail, and who was called Ferguson. He saw his own name; read the story of how the stranger had eclipsed his feat by putting six bullets into the can.

He dropped the page to the rock and looked up at Miss Radford with a short laugh.

"So that's what you're writin'?" he sneered. "You're writin' somethin' that really happened. You're even writin' the real names an' tellin' how Stafford's stray-man butted in an' beat me shootin'. You knowin' this shows that him an' you has been travelin' pretty close together."

For an instant Miss Radford forgot her anger. Her eyes snapped with a sudden interest.

"Were you the man who hit the can five times?" she questioned, unable to conceal her eagerness.

She saw a flush slowly mount to his face. Evidently he had said more than he had intended.

"Well, if I am?" he returned, his lips writhing in a sneer. "Him beatin' me shootin' that way don't prove nothin'."

She was now becoming convinced of her cleverness. From Ben's description of the man who had won the shooting match she had been able to lead Ferguson to the admission that he had been the central character in that incident, and now it had transpired that Leviatt was the man he had beaten. This had been the way she had written it in the story. So far the plot that had been born of her imagination had proved to be the story of a real occurrence.

She had counted upon none but imaginary characters,—though she had determined to clothe these with reality through study—but now, she had discovered, she had been the chronicler of a real incident, and two of her characters had been pitted against each other in a contest in which there had been enough bitterness to provide the animus necessary to carry them through succeeding pages, ready and willing to fly at each other's throats. She was not able to conceal her satisfaction over the discovery, and when she looked at Leviatt again she smiled broadly.

"That confession explains a great many things," she said, stooping to recover the page that he had dropped beside her upon the rock.

"Meanin' what?" he questioned, his eyes glittering evilly.

"Meaning that I now know why you are not friendly toward Mr. Ferguson," she returned. "I heard that he beat you in the shooting match," she went on tauntingly, "and then when you insulted him afterwards, he talked very plainly to you."

The moment she had spoken she realized that her words had hurt him, for he paled and his eyes narrowed venomously. But his voice was cold and steady.

"Was Mr. Ferguson tellin' you that?" he inquired, succeeding in placing ironic emphasis upon the prefix.

She was arranging the contents of her hand bag and she did not look up as she answered him.

"That is my business," she returned quietly. "But I don't mind telling you that the man who told me about the occurrence would not lie about it."

"It's nice that you've got such a heap of faith in him," he sneered.

It was plain to her that he thought Ferguson had told her about the shooting match, and it was equally plain that he still harbored evil thoughts against the stray-man. And also, he suspected that something more than mere friendship existed between her and Ferguson. She had long hoped that one day she might be given the opportunity of meeting in person a man whose soul was consumed with jealousy, in order that she might be able to gain some impressions of the intensity of his passion. This seemed to be her opportunity. Therefore she raised her chin a little and looked at him with a tantalizing smile.

"Of course I have faith in him," she declared, with a slight, biting emphasis. "I believe in him—absolutely."

She saw his lips twitch. "Sure," he sneered, "you was just beginnin' to believe in him that day when you was holdin' hands with him—just about here. I reckon he was enjoyin' himself."

She started, but smiled immediately. "So you saw that?" she inquired, knowing that he had, but taking a keen delight in seeing that he still remembered. But this conversation was becoming too personal; she had no desire to argue this point with him, even to get an impression of the depth of his passion, so she gathered up her belongings and prepared to depart. But he stepped deliberately in front of her, barring the way of escape. His face was aflame with passion.

"I seen him holdin' your hand," he said, his voice trembling; "I seen that he was holdin' it longer than he had any right. An' I seen you pull your hand away when you thought I was lookin' at you. I reckon you've taken a shine to him; he's the kind that the women like—with his slick ways an' smooth palaver—an' his love makin'." He laughed with his lips only, his eyes narrowed to glittering pin points. She had not thought that jealousy could make a person half so repulsive.

"If you're lovin' him," he continued, leaning toward her, his muscles tense, his lips quivering with a passion that he was no longer able to repress, "I'm tellin' you that you're wastin' your time. You wouldn't think so much of him if you knowed that he come here—"

Leviatt had become aware that Miss Radford was not listening; that she was no longer looking at him, but at something behind him. At the instant he became aware of this he turned sharply in his tracks, his right hand falling swiftly to his holster. Not over half a dozen paces distant stood Ben Radford, gravely watching.

"Mebbe you folks are rehearsing a scene from that story," he observed quietly. "I wasn't intending to interrupt, but I heard loud talking and I thought mebbe it wasn't anything private. So I just got off my horse and climbed up here, to satisfy my curiosity."

Leviatt's hand fell away from the holster, a guilty grin overspreading his face. "I reckon we wasn't rehearsin' any scene," he said, trying to make the words come easily. "I was just tellin' your sister that—"

Miss Radford laughed banteringly. "You have spoiled a chapter in my book, Ben," she declared with pretended annoyance; "Mr. Leviatt had just finished proposing to me and was at the point where he was supposed to speak bitter words about his rival." She laughed again, gazing at Leviatt with mocking eyes. "Of course, I shall never be able to tell my readers what he might have said, for you appeared at a most inopportune time. But he has taught me a great deal—much more, in fact, than I ever expected from him."

She bowed mockingly. "I am very, very much obliged to you, Mr. Leviatt," she said, placing broad emphasis upon her words. "I promise to try and make a very interesting character of you—there were times when you were most dramatic."

She bowed to Leviatt and flashed a dazzling smile at her brother. Then she walked past Leviatt, picked her way daintily over the loose stones on the hillside, and descended to the level where she had tethered her pony. Ben stood grinning admiringly after her as she mounted and rode out into the flat. Then he turned to Leviatt, soberly contemplating him.

"I don't think you were rehearsing for the book," he said quietly, an undercurrent of humor in his voice.

"She was funnin' me," returned Leviatt, his face reddening.

"I reckon she was," returned Ben dryly. "She's certainly some clever at handing it to a man." He smiled down into the flat, where Miss Radford could still be seen, riding toward the cabin. "Looks as though she wasn't quite ready to change her name to 'Leviatt'," he grinned.

But there was no humor in Leviatt's reflections. He stood for a moment, looking down into the flat, the expression of his face morose and sullen. Ben's bantering words only added fuel to the flame of rage and disappointment that was burning fiercely in his heart. Presently the hard lines of his lips disappeared and he smiled craftily.

"She's about ready to change her name," he said. "Only she ain't figgerin' that it's goin' to be Leviatt."

"You're guessing now," returned Ben sharply.

Leviatt laughed oddly. "I reckon I ain't doin' any guessin'," he returned. "You've been around her a heap an' been seein' her consid'able, but you ain't been usin' your eyes."

"Meaning what?" demanded Ben, an acid-like coldness in his voice.

"Meanin' that if you'd been usin' your eyes you'd have seen that she's some took up with Stafford's new stray-man."

"Well," returned Ben, "she's her own boss. If she's made friends with Ferguson that's her business." He laughed. "She's certainly clever," he added, "and mebbe she's got her own notion as to why she's made friends with him. She's told me that she's goin' to make him a character in the book she's writing. Likely she's stringing him."

"I reckon she ain't stringin' him," declared Leviatt. "A girl ain't doin' much stringin' when she's holdin' a man's hand an' blushin' when somebody ketches her at it."

There was a slight sneer in Leviatt's voice which drew a sharp glance from Radford. For an instant his face clouded and he was about to make a sharp reply. But his face cleared immediately and he smiled.

"I'm banking on her being able to take care of herself," he returned. "Her holding Ferguson's hand proves nothing. Likely she was trying to get an impression—she's always telling me that. But she's running her own game, and if she is stringing Ferguson that's her business, and if she thinks a good bit of him that's her business, too. If a man ain't jealous, he might be able to see that Ferguson ain't a half bad sort of a man."

An evil light leaped into Leviatt's eyes. He turned and faced Radford, words coming from his lips coldly and incisively. "When you interrupted me," he said, "I was goin' to tell your sister about Ferguson. Mebbe if I tell you what I was goin' to tell her it'll make you see things some different. A while ago Stafford was wantin' to hire a gunfighter." He shot a significant glance at Radford, who returned it steadily. "I reckon you know what he wanted a gunfighter for. He got one. His name's Ferguson. He's gettin' a hundred dollars a month for the season, to put Ben Radford out of business!"

The smile had gone from Radford's face; his lips were tightly closed, his eyes cold and alert.

"You lying about Ferguson because you think he's friendly with Mary?" he questioned quietly.

Leviatt's right hand dropped swiftly to his holster. But Radford laughed harshly. "Quit it!" he said sharply. "I ain't sayin' you're a liar, but what you've said makes you liable to be called that until you've proved you ain't. How do you know Ferguson's been hired to put me out of business?"

Leviatt laughed. "Stafford an' me went to Dry Bottom to get a gunfighter. I shot a can in the street in front of the Silver Dollar so's Stafford would be able to get a line on anyone tryin' to beat my game. Ferguson done it an' Stafford hired him."

Radford's gaze was level and steady. "Then you've knowed right along that he was lookin' for me," he said coldly. "Why didn't you say something about it before. You've been claiming to be my friend."

Leviatt flushed, shifting uneasily from one foot to the other, but watching Radford with alert and suspicious glances. "Why," he returned shortly, "I'm range boss for the Two Diamond an' I ain't hired to tell what I know. I reckon you'd think I was a hell of a man to be tellin' things that I ain't got no right to tell."

"But you're telling it now," returned Radford, his eyes narrowing a little.

"Yes," returned Leviatt quietly, "I am. An' you're callin' me a liar for it. But I'm tellin' you to wait. Mebbe you'll tumble. I reckon you ain't heard how Ferguson's been tellin' the boys that he went down to your cabin one night claimin' to have been bit by a rattler, because he wanted to get acquainted with you an' pot you some day when you wasn't expectin' it. An' then after he'd stayed all night in your cabin he was braggin' to the boys that he reckoned on makin' a fool of your sister. Oh, he's some slick!" he concluded, a note of triumph in his voice.

Radford started, his face paling a little. He had thought it strange that an experienced plainsman—as Ferguson appeared to be—should have been bitten by a rattler in the manner he had described. And then he had been hanging around the—

"Mebbe you might think it's onusual for Stafford to hire a two-gun man to look after strays," broke in Leviatt at this point. "Two-gun men ain't takin' such jobs regular," he insinuated. "Stray-men is usual low-down, mean, ornery cusses which ain't much good for anything else, an' so they spend their time mopin' around, doin' work that ain't fit for any puncher to do."

Radford had snapped himself erect, his lips straightening. He suddenly held out a hand to Leviatt. "I'm thanking you," he said steadily. "It's rather late for you to be telling me, but I think it's come in time anyway. I'm watching him for a little while, and if things are as you say—" He broke off, his voice filled with a significant grimness. "So-long," he added.

He turned and descended the slope of the hill. An instant later Leviatt saw him loping his pony toward the cabin. For a few minutes Leviatt gazed after him, his eyes alight with satisfaction. Then he, too, descended the slope of the hill and mounted his pony.

CHAPTER XVII

A BREAK IN THE STORY

Mary Radford had found the day too beautiful to remain indoors and so directly after dinner she had caught up her pony and was off for a ride through the cottonwood. She had been compelled to catch up the pony herself, for of late Ben had been neglectful of this duty. Until the last week or so he had always caught her pony and placed the saddle on it before leaving in the morning, assuring her that if she did not ride during his absence the pony would not suffer through being saddled and bridled. But within the last week she thought she detected a change in Ben's manner. He seemed preoccupied and glum, falling suddenly into a taciturnity broken only by brief periods during which he condescended to reply to her questions with—it seemed—grudging monosyllables.

Several times, too, she had caught him watching her with furtive glances in which, she imagined, she detected a glint of speculation. But of this she was not quite sure, for when she bluntly questioned him concerning his moods he had invariably given her an evasive reply. Fearing that there might have been a recurrence of the old trouble with the Two Diamond manager—about which he had told her during her first days at the cabin—she ventured a question. He had grimly assured her that he anticipated no further trouble in that direction. So, unable to get a direct reply from him she had decided that perhaps he would speak when the time came, and so she had ceased questioning.

In spite of his negligence regarding the pony, she had not given up her rides. Nor had she neglected to give a part of each morning to the story.

The work of gradually developing her hero's character had been an absorbing task; times when she lingered over the pages of the story she found herself wondering whether she had sounded the depths of his nature. She knew, at least, that she had made him attractive, for as he moved among her pages, she—who should have been satiated with him because of being compelled to record his every word and movement—found his magnetic personality drawing her applause, found that he haunted her dreams, discovered one day that her waking moments were filled with thoughts of him.

But of late she had begun to suspect that her interest in him was not all on account of the story; there were times when she sat long thinking of him, seeing him, watching the lights and shadows of expression come and go in his face. Somewhere between the real Ferguson and the man who was impersonating him in her story was an invisible line that she could not trace. There were times when she could not have told whether the character she admired belonged to the real or the unreal.

She was thinking much of this to-day while she rode into the subdued light of the cottonwood. Was she, absorbed in the task of putting a real character in her story, to confess that her interest in him was not wholly the interest of the artist who sees the beauties and virtues of a model only long enough to paint them into the picture? The blushes came when she suddenly realized that her interest was not wholly professional, that she had lately lingered long over her model, at times when she had not been thinking of the story at all.

Then, too, she had considered her friends in the East. What would they say if they knew of her friendship with the Two Diamond strayman? The standards of Eastern civilization were not elastic enough to include the man whom she had come to know so well, who had strode as boldly into her life as he had strode into her story, with his steady, serene eyes, his picturesque rigging, and his two guns, their holsters tied so suggestively and forebodingly down. Would her friends be able to see the romance in him? Would they be able to estimate him according to the standards of the world in which he lived, in which he moved so gracefully?

She was aware that, measured by Eastern standards, Ferguson fell far short of the average in those things that combine to produce the polished gentleman. Yet she was also aware that these things were mere accomplishments, a veneer acquired through constant practice—and that usually the person known as "gentleman" could not be distinguished by these things at all—that the real "gentleman" could be known only through the measure of his quiet and genuine consideration and unfailing Christian virtues.

As she rode through the cottonwood, into that deep solitude which brings with it a mighty reverence for nature and a solemn desire for communion with the soul—that solitude in which all affectation disappears and man is face to face with his Maker—she tried to think of Ferguson in an Eastern drawing room, attempting a sham courtesy, affecting mannerisms that more than once had brought her own soul into rebellion. But she could not get him into the imaginary picture. He did not belong there; it seemed that she was trying to force a living figure into a company of mechanical puppets. And so they were—puppets who answered to the pulling strings of precedent and established convention.

But at the same time she knew that this society which she affected to despise would refuse to accept him; that if by any chance he should be given a place in it he would be an object of ridicule, or at the least passive contempt. The world did not want originality; would not welcome in its drawing room the free, unaffected child of nature. No, the world wanted pretense, imitation. It frowned upon truth and applauded the sycophant.

She was not even certain that if she succeeded in making Ferguson a real living character the world would be interested in him. But she had reached that state of mind in which she cared very little about the world's opinion. She, at least, was interested in him.

Upon the same afternoon—for there is no rule for the mere incidents of life—Ferguson loped his pony through the shade of the cottonwood. He was going to visit the cabin in Bear Flat. Would she be at home? Would she be glad to see him? He could not bring his mind to give him an affirmative answer to either of these questions.

But of one thing he was certain—she had treated him differently from the other Two Diamond men who had attempted to win her friendship. Was he to think then that she cared very little whether he came to the cabin or not? He smiled over his pony's mane at the thought. He could not help but see that she enjoyed his visits.

When he rode up to the cabin he found it deserted, but with a smile he remounted Mustard and set out over the river trail, through the cottonwood. He was sure that he would find her on the hill in the flat, and when he had reached the edge of the cottonwood opposite the hill he saw her.

When she heard the clatter of his pony's hoofs she turned and saw him, waving a hand at him.

"I reckoned on findin' you here," he said when he came close enough to be heard.

She shyly made room for him beside her on the rock, but there was mischief in her eye. "It seems impossible to hide from you," she said with a pretense of annoyance.

He laughed as he came around the edge of the rock and sat near her. "Was you really tryin' to hide?" he questioned. "Because if you was," he continued, "you hadn't ought to have got up on this hill—where I could see you without even lookin' for you."

"But of course you were not looking for me," she observed quietly.

He caught her gaze and held it—steadily. "I reckon I was lookin' for you," he said.

"Why—why," she returned, suddenly fearful that something had happened to Ben—"is anything wrong?"

He smiled. "Nothin' is wrong," he returned. "But I wanted to talk to you, an' I expected to find you here."

There was a gentleness in his voice that she had not heard before, and a quiet significance to his words that made her eyes droop away from his with slight confusion. She replied without looking at him.

"But I came here to write," she said.

He gravely considered her, drawing one foot up on the rock and clasping his hands about the knee. "I've thought a lot about that book," he declared with a trace of embarrassment, "since you told me that you was goin' to put real men an' women in it. I expect you've made them do the things that you've wanted them to do an' made them say what you wanted them to say. That part is right an' proper—there wouldn't be any sense of anyone writin' a book unless they could put into it what they thought was right. But what's been botherin' me is this; how can you tell whether the things you've made them say is what they would have said if they'd had any chance to talk? An' how can you tell what their feelin's would be when you set them doin' somethin'?"

She laughed. "That is a prerogative which the writer assumes without question," she returned. "The author of a novel makes his characters think and act as the author himself imagines he would act in the same circumstances."

He looked at her with amused eyes. "That's just what I was tryin' to get at," he said. "You've put me into your book, an' you've made me do an' say things out of your mind. But you don't know for sure whether I would have done an' said things just like you've wrote them. Mebbe if I would have had somethin' to say I wouldn't have done things your way at all."

"I am sure you would," she returned positively.

"Well, now," he returned smiling, "you're speakin' as though you was pretty certain about it. You must have wrote a whole lot of the story."

"It is two-thirds finished," she returned with a trace of satisfaction in her voice which did not escape him.

"An' you've got all your characters doin' an' thinkin' things that you think they ought to do?" His eyes gleamed craftily. "You got a man an' a girl in it?"

"Of course."

"An' they're goin' to love one another?"

"No other outcome is popular with novel readers," she returned.

He rocked back and forth, his eyes languidly surveying the rim of hills in the distance.

"I expect that outcome is popular in real life too," he observed. "Nobody ever hears about it when it turns out some other way."

"I expect love is always a popular subject," she returned smiling.

His eyes were still languid, his gaze still on the rim of distant hills.

"You got any love talk in there—between the man an' the girl?" he questioned.

"Of course."

"That's mighty interestin'," he returned. "I expect they do a good bit of mushin'?"

"They do not talk extravagantly," she defended.

"Then I expect it must be pretty good," he returned. "I don't like mushy love stories." And now he turned and looked fairly at her. "Of course," he said slyly, "I don't know whether it's necessary or not, but I've been thinkin' that to write a good love story the writer ought to be in love. Whoever was writin' would know more about how it feels to be in love."

She admired the cleverness with which he had led her up to this point, but she was not to be trapped. She met his eyes fairly.

"I am sure it is not necessary for the writer to be in love," she said quietly but positively. "I flatter myself that my love scenes are rather real, and I have not found it necessary to love anyone."

This reply crippled him instantly. "Well, now," he said, eyeing her, she thought, a bit reproachfully, "that comes pretty near stumpin' me. But," he added, a subtle expression coming again into his eyes, "you say you've got only two-thirds finished. Mebbe you'll be in love before you get it all done. An' then mebbe you'll find that you didn't get it right an' have to do it all over again. That would sure be too bad, when you could have got in love an' wrote it real in the first place."

"I don't think that I shall fall in love," she said laughing.

He looked quickly at her, suddenly grave. "I wouldn't want to think you meant that," he said.

"Why?" she questioned in a low voice, her laughter subdued by his earnestness.

"Why," he said steadily, as though stating a perfectly plain fact, "I've thought right along that you liked me. Of course I ain't been fool enough to think that you loved me"—and now he reddened a little—, "but I don't deny that I've hoped that you would."

"Oh, dear!" she laughed; "and so you have planned it all out! And I was hoping that you would not prove so deep as that. You know," she went on, "you promised me a long while ago that you would not fall in love with me."

"I don't reckon that I said that," he returned. "I told you that I wasn't goin' to get fresh. I reckon I ain't fresh now. But I expect I couldn't help lovin' you—I've done that since the first day."

She could not stop the blushes—they would come. And so would that thrilling, breathless exultation. No man had ever talked to her like this; no man had ever made her feel quite as she felt at this moment. She turned a crimson face to him.

"But you hadn't any right to love me," she declared, feeling sure that she had been unable to make him understand that she meant to rebuke him. Evidently he did not understand that she meant to do that, for he unclasped his hand from his knee and came closer to her, standing at the edge of the rock, one hand resting upon it.

"Of course I didn't have any right," he said gravely, "but I loved you just the same. There's been some things in my life that I couldn't help doin'. Lovin' you is one. I expect that you'll think I'm pretty fresh, but I've been thinkin' a whole lot about you an' I've got to tell you. You ain't like the women I've been used to. An' I reckon I ain't just the kind of man you've been acquainted with all your life. You've been used to seein' men who was all slicked up an' clever. I expect them kind of men appeal to any woman. I ain't claimin' to be none of them clever kind, but I've been around quite a little an' I ain't never done anything that I'm ashamed of. I can't offer you a heap, but if you—"

She had looked up quickly, her cheeks burning.

"Please don't," she pleaded, rising and placing a hand on his arm, gripping it tightly. "I have known for a long time, but I—I wanted to be sure." He could not suspect that she had only just now begun to realize that she was in danger of yielding to him and that the knowledge frightened her.

"You wanted to be sure?" he questioned, his face clouding. "What is it that you wanted to be sure of?"

"Why," she returned, laughing to hide her embarrassment, "I wanted to be sure that you loved me!"

"Well, you c'n be sure now," he said.

"I believe I can," she laughed. "And," she continued, finding it difficult to pretend seriousness, "knowing what I do will make writing so much easier."

His face clouded again. "I don't see what your writin' has got to do with it," he said.

"You don't?" she demanded, her eyes widening with pretended surprise. "Why, don't you see that I wanted to be sure of your love so that I might be able to portray a real love scene in my story?"

He did not reply instantly, but folded his arms over his chest and stood looking at her. In his expression was much reproach and not a little disappointment. The hopes that had filled his dreams had been ruined by her frivolous words; he saw her at this moment a woman who had trifled with him, who had led him cleverly on to a declaration of love that she might in the end sacrifice him to her art. But in this moment, when he might have been excused for exhibiting anger; for heaping upon her the bitter reproaches of an outraged confidence, he was supremely calm. The color fled from his face, leaving it slightly pale, and his eyes swam with a deep feeling that told of the struggle that he was making.

"I didn't think you'd do it, ma'am," he said finally, a little hoarsely. "But I reckon you know your own business best." He smiled slightly. "I don't think there's any use of you an' me meetin' again—I don't want to be goin' on, bein' a dummy man that you c'n watch. But I'm glad to have amused you some an' I have enjoyed myself, talkin' to you. But I reckon you've done what you wanted to do, an' so I'll be gettin' along."

He smiled grimly and with an effort turned and walked around the corner of the rock, intending to descend the hill and mount his pony. But as he passed around to the side of the rock he heard her voice:

"Wait, please," she said in a scarcely audible voice.

He halted, looking gravely at her from the opposite side of the rock.

"You wantin' to get somethin' more for your story?" he asked.

She turned and looked over her shoulder at him, her eyes luminous with a tell-tale expression, her face crimson. "Why," she said smiling at him, "do you really think that I could be so mean?"

He was around the rock again in half a dozen steps and standing above her, his eyes alight, his lips parted slightly with surprise and eagerness.

"Do you mean that you wantin' to make sure that I loved you wasn't all for the sake of the story?" he demanded rapidly.

Her eyes drooped away from his. "Didn't you tell me that a writer should be in love in order to be able to write of it?" she asked, her face averted.

"Yes." He was trembling a little and leaning toward her. In this position he caught her low reply.

"I think my love story will be real," she returned. "I have learned—" But whatever she might have wanted to add was smothered when his arms closed tightly about her.

A little later she drew a deep breath and looked up at him with moist, eloquent eyes.

"Perhaps I *shall* have to change the story a little," she said.

He drew her head to his shoulder, one hand caressing her hair. "If you do," he said smiling, "don't have the hero thinkin' that the girl is makin' a fool of him." He drew her close. "That cert'nly was a mighty bad minute you give me," he added.

CHAPTER XVIII

THE DIM TRAIL.

A shadow fell upon the rock. Ferguson turned his head and looked toward the west, where the sun had already descended over the mountains.

"Why it's sundown!" he said, smiling into Miss Radford's eyes. "I reckon the days must be gettin' shorter."

"The happy days are always short," she returned, blushing. He kissed her for this. For a while they sat, watching together the vari-colors swimming in the sky. They sat close together, saying little, for mere words are sometimes inadequate. In a little time the colors faded, the mountain peaks began to throw sombre shades; twilight—gray and cold—settled suddenly into the flat. Then Miss Radford raised her head from Ferguson's shoulder and sighed.

"Time to go home," she said.

"Yes, time," he returned. "I'm ridin' down that far with you."

They rose and clambered down the hillside and he helped her into the saddle. Then he mounted Mustard and rode across the flat beside her.

Darkness had fallen when they rode through the clearing near the cabin and dismounted from their ponies at the door. The light from the kerosene lamp shone in a dim stream from the kitchen door and within they saw dishes on the table with cold food. Ferguson stood beside his pony while Miss Radford went in and explored the cabin. She came to the door presently, shading her eyes to look out into the darkness.

"Ben has been here and gone," she said. "He can't be very far away. Won't you come in?"

He laughed. "I don't think I'll come in," he returned. "This lover business is new to me, an' I wouldn't want Ben to come back an' ketch me blushin' an' takin' on."

"But he has to know," she insisted, laughing.

"Sure," he said, secure in the darkness, "but you tell him."

"I won't!" she declared positively, stamping a foot.

"Then I reckon he won't get told," he returned quietly.

"Well, then," she said, laughing, "I suppose that is settled."

She came out to the edge of the porch, away from the door, where the stream of light from within could not search them out, and there they took leave of one another, she going back into the cabin and he mounting Mustard and riding away in the darkness.

He was in high spirits, for he had much to be thankful for. As he rode through the darkness, skirting the cottonwood in the flat, he allowed his thoughts to wander. His refusal to enter the cabin had not been a mere whim; he intended on the morrow to seek out Ben and tell him. He had not wanted to tell him with her looking on to make the situation embarrassing for him.

When he thought of how she had fooled him by making it appear that she had led him on for the purpose of getting material for her love story, he was moved to silent mirth. "But I cert'nly didn't see anything funny in it while she was puttin' it on," he told himself, as he rode.

He had not ridden more than a quarter of a mile from the cabin, and was passing a clump of heavy shrubbery, when a man rose suddenly out of the shadows beside the trail. Startled, Mustard reared, and then seeing that the apparition was merely a man, he came quietly down and halted, shaking his head sagely. Ferguson's right hand had dropped swiftly to his right holster, but was raised again instantly as the man's voice came cold and steady:

"Get your hands up—quick!"

Ferguson's hands were raised, but he gave no evidence of fear or excitement. Instead, he leaned forward, trying, in the dim light, to see the man's face. The latter still stood in the shadows. But now he advanced a little toward Ferguson, and the stray-man caught his breath sharply. But when he spoke his voice was steady.

"Why, it's Ben Radford," he said.

"That's just who it is," returned Radford. "I've been waitin' for you."

"That's right clever of you," returned Ferguson, drawling his words a little. He was puzzled over this unusual occurrence, but his face did not betray this. "You was wantin' to see me then," he added.

"You're keen," returned Radford, sneering slightly.

Ferguson's face reddened. "I ain't no damn fool," he said sharply. "An' I don't like holdin' my hands up like this. I reckon whatever you're goin' to do you ought to do right quick."

"I'm figuring to be quick," returned Radford shortly. "Ketch hold of your guns with the tips of one finger and one thumb and drop them. Don't hit any rocks and don't try any monkey business."

He waited until Ferguson had dropped one gun. And then, knowing that the stray-man usually wore two weapons, he continued sharply: "I'm waiting for the other one."

Ferguson laughed. "Then you'll be waitin' a long time. There ain't any 'other one. Broke a spring yesterday an' sent it over to Cimarron to get it fixed up. You c'n have it when it comes back," he added with a touch of sarcasm, "if you're carin' to wait that long."

Radford did not reply, but came around to Ferguson's left side and peered at the holster. It was empty. Then he looked carefully at the stray-man's waist for signs that a weapon might have been concealed between the waist-band and the trousers—in front. Then, apparently satisfied, he stepped back, his lips closed grimly.

"Get off your horse," he ordered.

Ferguson laughed as he swung down. "Anything to oblige a friend," he said, mockingly.

The two men were now not over a yard apart, and at Ferguson's word Radford's face became inflamed with wrath. "I don't think I'm a friend of yours," he sneered coldly; "I ain't making friends with every damned sneak that crawls around the country, aiming to shoot a man in the back." He raised his voice, bitter with sarcasm. "You're thinking that you're pretty slick," he said; "that all you have to do in this country is to hang around till you get a man where you want him and then bore him. But you've got to the end of your rope. You ain't going to shoot anyone around here.

"I'm giving you a chance to say what you've got to say and then I'm going to fill you full of lead and plant you over in the cottonwood—in a place where no one will ever be able to find you—not even Stafford. I'd have shot you off your horse when you come around the bend," he continued coldly, "but I wanted you to know who was doing it and that the man that did it knowed what you come here to do." He poised his pistol menacingly. "You got anything to say?" he inquired.

Ferguson looked steadily from the muzzle of the poised weapon to Radford's frowning eyes. Then he smiled grimly.

"Some one's been talkin'," he said evenly. He calmly crossed his arms over his chest, the right hand slipping carelessly under the left side of his vest. Then he rocked slowly back and forth on his heels and toes. "Someone's been tellin' you a pack of lies," he added. "I reckon you've wondered, if I was goin' to shoot you in the back, that I ain't done it long ago. You're admittin' that I've had some chance."

Radford sneered. "I ain't wondering why you ain't done it before," he said. "Mebbe it was because you're too white livered. Mebbe you thought you didn't see your chance. I ain't worrying none about why you didn't do it. But you ain't going to get another chance." The weapon came to a foreboding level.

Ferguson laughed grimly, but there was an ironic quality in his voice that caught Radford's ear. It seemed to Radford that the stray-man knew that he was near death, and yet some particular phase of the situation appealed to his humor—grim though it was. It came out when the stray-man spoke.

"You've been gassin' just now about shootin' people in the back—sayin' that I've been thinkin' of doin' it. But I reckon you ain't thought a lot about the way you're intendin' to put me out of business. I was wonderin' if it made any difference—shootin' a man in the back or shootin' him when he ain't got any guns. I expect a man that's shot when he ain't got guns would be just as dead as a man that's shot in the back, wouldn't he?"

He laughed again, his eyes gleaming in the dim light. "That's the reason I ain't scared a heap," he said. "From what I know about you you ain't the man to shoot another without givin' him a chance. An' you're givin' me a chance to talk. I ain't goin' to do any prayin'. I reckon that's right?"

Radford shifted his feet uneasily. He could not have told at that moment whether or not he had intended to murder Ferguson. He had waylaid him with that intention, utterly forgetful that by shooting the stray-man he would be committing the very crime which he had accused Ferguson of contemplating. The muzzle of his weapon drooped uncertainly.

"Talk quick!" he said shortly.

Ferguson grinned. "I'm takin' my time," he returned. "There ain't any use of bein' in such an awful hurry—time don't amount to much when a man's talkin' for his life. I ain't askin' who told you what you've said about me—I've got a pretty clear idea who it was. I've had to tell a man pretty plain that my age has got its growth an' I don't think that man is admirin' me much for bein' told. But if he's wantin' to have me put out of business he's goin' to do the job himself—Ben Radford ain't doin' it."

While he had been talking he had contrived to throw the left side of his vest open, and his right hand was exposed in the dim light—a heavy six-shooter gleaming forebodingly in it. His arms were still crossed, but as he talked he had turned a very little and now the muzzle of the weapon was at a level—trained fairly upon Radford's breast. And then came Ferguson's voice again, quiet, cold, incisive.

"If there's goin' to be any shootin', Ben, there'll be two of us doin' it. Don't be afraid that you'll beat me to it." And he stared grimly over the short space that separated them.

For a full minute neither man moved a muscle. Silence—a premonitory silence—fell over them as they stood, each with a steady finger dragging uncertainly upon the trigger of his weapon. An owl hooted in the cottonwood nearby; other noises of the night reached their ears. Unaware of this crisis Mustard grazed unconcernedly at a distance.

Then Radford's weapon wavered a little and dropped to his side.

"This game's too certain," he said.

Ferguson laughed, and his six-shooter disappeared as mysteriously as it had appeared. "I thought I'd be able to make you see the point," he said. "It don't always pay to be in too much of a hurry to do a thing," he continued gravely. "An' I reckon I've proved that someone's been lying about me. If I'd wanted to shoot you I could have done it quite a spell ago—I had you covered just as soon as I crossed my arms. You'd never knowed about it. That I didn't shoot proves that whoever told you I was after you has been romancin'." He laughed.

"An' now I'm tellin' you another thing that I was goin' to tell you about to-morrow. Mebbe you'll want to shoot me for that. But if you do I expect you'll have a woman to fight. Me an' Mary has found that we're of one mind about a thing. We're goin' to hook up into a double harness. I reckon when I'm your brother-in-law you won't be so worried about shootin' me."

Radford's astonishment showed for a moment in his eyes as his gaze met the stray-man's. Then they drooped guiltily.

"Well I'm a damn fool!" he said finally. "I might have knowed that Mary wouldn't get afoul of any man who was thinkin' of doing dirt to me." He suddenly extended a hand. "You shakin'?" he said.

Ferguson took the hand, gripping it tightly. Neither man spoke. Then Radford suddenly unclasped his hand and turned, striding rapidly up the trail toward the cabin.

For a moment Ferguson stood, looking after him with narrowed, friendly eyes. Then he walked to Mustard, threw the bridle rein over the pommel of the saddle, mounted, and was off at a rapid lope toward the Two Diamond.

CHAPTER XIX

THE SHOT IN THE DARK

Now that Mary Radford had obtained experience for the love scene in her story it might be expected that on returning to the cabin she would get out her writing materials and attempt to transcribe the emotions that had beset her during the afternoon, but she did nothing of the kind. After Ferguson's departure she removed her riding garments, walked several times around the interior of the cabin, and for a long time studied her face in the looking glass. Yes, she discovered the happiness shining out of the glass. Several times, standing before the glass, she attempted to keep the lines of her face in repose, and though she almost succeeded in doing this she could not control her eyes—they simply would gleam with the light that seemed to say to her: "You may deceive people by making a mask of your face, but the eyes are the windows of the soul and through them people will see your secret."

Ben hadn't eaten much, she decided, as she seated herself at the table, after pouring a cup of tea. Before she had finished her meal she had begun to wonder over his absence—it was not his custom to go away in the night. She thought he might have gone to the corral, or might even be engaged in some small task in the stable. So after completing her meal she rose and went to the door, looking out.

There was no moon, only the starlight, but in this she was able to distinguish objects in the clearing, and if Ben had been working about anywhere she must have noticed him. She returned to the table and sat there long, pondering. Then she rose, heated some water, and washed and dried the dishes. Then she swept the kitchen floor and tidied things up a bit, returning to the door when all was complete.

Still no signs that Ben was anywhere in the vicinity. She opened the screen door and went out upon the porch, leaning against one of the slender posts. For a long time she stood thus, listening to the indescribable noises of the night. This was only the second time since she had been with Ben that he had left her alone at night, and a slight chill stole over her as she watched the dense shadows beyond the clearing, shadows that seemed suddenly dismal and foreboding. She had loved the silence, but now suddenly it too seemed too deep, too solemn to be real. She shuddered, and with some unaccountable impulse shrank back against the screen door, one hand upon it, ready to throw it open. In this position she stood for a few minutes, and then from somewhere in the flat came a slight sound—and then, after a short interval, another.

She shrank back again, a sudden fear chilling her, her hands clasped over her breast.

"Someone is shooting," she said aloud.

She waited long for a repetition of the sounds. But she did not hear them again. Tremblingly she returned to the cabin and resumed her chair at the table, fighting against a growing presentiment that something had gone wrong with Ben. But she could not have told from what direction the sounds had come, and so it would have been folly for her to ride out to investigate. And so for an hour she sat at the table, cringing away from the silence, starting at intervals, when her imagination tricked her into the belief that sound had begun.

And then presently she became aware that there was sound. In the vast silence beyond the cabin door something had moved. She was on her feet instantly, her senses alert. Her fear had left her. Her face was pale, but her lips closed grimly as she went to the rack behind the door and took down a rifle that Ben always kept there. Then she turned the lamp low and cautiously stepped to the door.

A pony whinnied, standing with ears erect at the edge of the porch. In a crumpled heap on the ground lay a man. She caught her breath sharply, but in the next instant was out and bending over him. With a strength that seemed almost beyond her shy dragged the limp form to the door where the light from the lamp shone upon it.

"Ben!" she said sharply. "What has happened?" She shook him slightly, calling again to him.

Aroused, he opened his eyes, recognized her, and raised himself painfully upon one elbow, smiling weakly.

"It ain't anything, sis," he said. "Creased in the back of the head. Knocked me cold. Mebbe my shoulder too—I ain't been able to lift my arm." He smiled again—grimly, though wearily. "From the back too. The damned sneak!"

Her eyes filled vengefully, and she leaned closer to him, her voice tense. "Who, Ben? Who did it?"

"Ferguson," he said sharply. And again, as his eyes closed: "The damned sneak."

She swayed dizzily and came very near dropping him to the porch floor. But no sound came from her, and presently when the dizziness had passed, she dragged him to the door, propped it open with a chair, and then dragged him on through the opening to the kitchen, and from there to one of the adjoining rooms. Then with pale face and determined lips she set about the work of taking care of Ben's wounds. The spot on the back of the head, she found, was a mere abrasion, as he had said. But his shoulder had been shattered, the bullet, she discovered, having passed clear through the fleshy part of the shoulder, after breaking one of the smaller bones.

Getting her scissors she clipped away the hair from the back of his head and sponged the wound and bandaged it, convinced that of itself it was not dangerous. Then she undressed him, and by the use of plenty of clear, cold water, a sponge, and some bandages, stopped the flow of blood in his shoulder and placed him in a comfortable position. He had very little fever, but she moved rapidly around him, taking his temperature, administering sedatives when he showed signs of restlessness, hovering over him constantly until the dawn began to come.

Soon after this he went off into a peaceful sleep, and, almost exhausted with her efforts and the excitement, she threw herself upon the floor beside his bed, sacrificing her own comfort that she might be near to watch should he need her. It was late in the afternoon when Radford opened his eyes to look out through the door that connected his room with the kitchen and saw his sister busying herself with the dishes. His mind was clear and he suffered very little pain. For a long time he lay, quietly watching her, while his thoughts went back to the meeting on the trail with Ferguson. Why hadn't he carried out his original intention of shooting the stray-man down from ambush? He had doubted Leviatt's word and had hesitated, wishing to give Ferguson the benefit of the doubt, and had received his reward in the shape of a bullet in the back—after practically making a peace pact with his intended victim.

He presently became aware that his sister was standing near him, and he looked up and smiled at her. Then in an instant she was kneeling beside him, admonishing him to quietness, smoothing his forehead, giving delighted little gasps over his improved condition. But in spite of her evident cheerfulness there was a suggestion of trouble swimming deep in her eyes; he could not help but see that she was making a brave attempt to hide her bitter disappointment over the turn things had taken. Therefore he was not surprised when, after she had attended to all his wants, she sank on her knees beside him.

"Ben," she said, trying to keep a quiver out of her voice, "are you sure it was Ferguson who shot you?"

He patted her hand tenderly and sympathetically with his uninjured one. "I'm sorry for you, Mary," he returned, "but there ain't any doubt about it." Then he told her of the warning he had received from Leviatt, and when he saw her lips curl at the mention of the Two Diamond range boss's name he smiled.

"I thought the same thing that you are thinking, Mary," he said. "And I didn't want to shoot Ferguson. But as things have turned out I wouldn't have been much wrong to have done it."

She raised her head from the coverlet. "Did you see him before he shot you?" she questioned eagerly.

"Just a little before," he returned. "I met him at a turn in the trail about half a mile from here. I made him get down off his horse and drop his guns. We had a talk, for I didn't want to shoot him until I was sure, and he talked so clever that I thought he was telling the truth. But he wasn't."

He told her about Ferguson's concealed pistol; how they had stood face to face with death between them, concluding: "By that time I had decided not to shoot him. But he didn't have the nerve to pull the trigger when he was looking at me. He waited until I'd got on my horse and was riding away. Then he sneaked up behind."

He saw her body shiver, and he caressed her hair slowly, telling her that he was sorry things had turned out so, and promising her that when he recovered he would bring the Two Diamond stray-man to a strict accounting—providing the latter didn't leave the country before. But he saw that his words had given her little comfort, for when an hour or so later he dropped off to sleep the last thing he saw was her seated at the table in the kitchen, her head bowed in her hands, crying softly.

"Poor little kid," he said, as sleep dimmed his eyes; "it looks as though this would be the end of *her* story."

CHAPTER XX

LOVE AND A RIFLE

Ferguson did not visit Miss Radford the next morning—he had seen Leviatt and Tucson depart from the ranchhouse, had observed the direction they took, and had followed them. For twenty miles he had kept them in sight, watching them with a stern patience that had brought its reward.

They had ridden twenty miles straight down the river, when Ferguson, concealed behind a ridge, saw them suddenly disappear into a little basin. Then he rode around the ridge, circled the rim of hills that surrounded the basin, and dismounting from his pony, crept through a scrub oak thicket to a point where he could look directly down upon them.

He was surprised into a subdued whistle. Below him in the basin was an adobe hut. He had been through this section of the country several times but had never before stumbled upon the hut. This was not remarkable, for situated as it was, in this little basin, hidden from sight by a serried line of hills and ridges among which no cowpuncher thought to travel—nor cared to—, the cabin was as safe from prying eyes as it was possible for a human habitation to be.

There was a small corral near the cabin, in which there were several steers, half a dozen cows, and perhaps twenty calves. As Ferguson's eyes took in the latter detail, they glittered with triumph. Not even the wildest stretch of the imagination could produce twenty calves from half a dozen cows.

But Ferguson did not need this evidence to convince him that the men who occupied the cabin were rustlers. Honest men did not find it necessary to live in a basin in the hills where they were shut in from sight of the open country. Cattle thieves did not always find it necessary to do so—unless they were men like these, who had no herds of their own among which to conceal their ill-gotten beasts. He was convinced that these men were migratory thieves, who operated upon the herds nearest them, remained until they had accumulated a considerable number of cattle, and then drove the entire lot to some favored friend who was not averse to running the risk of detection if through that risk he came into possession of easily earned money.

There were two of the men, beside Leviatt and Tucson—tall, rangy—looking their part. Ferguson watched them for half an hour, and then, convinced that he would gain nothing more by remaining there, he stealthily backed down the hillside to where his pony stood, mounted, and rode toward the river.

Late in the afternoon he entered Bear Flat, urged his pony at a brisk pace across it, and just before sundown drew rein in front of the Radford cabin. He dismounted and stepped to the edge of the porch, a smile of anticipation on his lips. The noise of his arrival brought Mary Radford to the door. She came out upon the porch, and he saw that her face was pale and her lips firmly set. Apparently something had gone amiss with her and he halted, looking at her questioningly.

"What's up?" he asked.

"You ought to know," she returned quietly.

"I ain't good at guessin' riddles," he returned, grinning at her.

"There is no riddle," she answered, still quietly. She came forward until she stood within two paces of him, her eyes meeting his squarely. "When you left here last night did you meet Ben on the trail?" she continued steadily.

He started, reddening a little. "Why, yes," he returned, wondering if Ben had told her what had been said at that meeting; "was he tellin' you about it?"

"Yes," she returned evenly, "he has been telling me about it. That should be sufficient for you. I am sorry that I ever met you. You should know why. If I were you I should not lose any time in getting away from here."

Her voice was listless, even flat, but there was a grim note in it that told that she was keeping her composure with difficulty. He laughed, thinking that since he had made the new agreement with the Two Diamond manager he had nothing to fear. "I reckon I ought to be scared," he returned, "but I ain't. An' I don't consider that I'm losin' any time."

Her lips curved sarcastically. "You have said something like that before," she told him, her eyes glittering scornfully. "You have a great deal of faith in your ability to fool people. But you have miscalculated this time.

"I know why you have come to the Two Diamond. I know what made you come over here so much. Of course I am partly to blame. You have fooled me as you have fooled everyone." She stood suddenly erect, her eyes flashing. "If you planned to kill my brother, why did you not have the manhood to meet him face to face?"

Ferguson flushed. Would it help his case to deny that he had thought of fooling her, that he never had any intention of shooting Ben? He thought not. Leviatt had poisoned her mind against him. He smiled grimly.

"Someone's been talkin'," he said quietly. "You'd be helpin' to make this case clear if you'd tell who it was."

"Someone has talked," she replied; "someone who knows. Why didn't you tell me that you came here to kill Ben? That you were hired by Stafford to do it?"

"Why, I didn't, ma'am," he protested, his face paling.

"You did!" She stamped one foot vehemently.

Ferguson's eyes drooped. "I came here to see if Ben was rustlin' cattle, ma'am," he confessed frankly. "But I wasn't intendin' to shoot him. Why, I've had lots of chances, an' I didn't do it. Ain't that proof enough?"

"No," she returned, her voice thrilling with a sudden, bitter irony, "you didn't shoot him. That is, you didn't shoot him while he was looking at you—when there was a chance that he might have given you as good as you sent. No, you didn't shoot him then—you waited until his back was turned. You—you coward!"

Ferguson's lips whitened. "You're talkin' extravagant, ma'am," he said coldly. "Somethin' is all mixed up. Has someone been shootin' Ben?"

She sneered, pinning him with a scornful, withering glance. "I expected that you would deny it," she returned. "That would be following out your policy of deception."

He leaned forward, his eyes wide with surprise. If she had not been laboring under the excitement of the incident she might have seen that his surprise was genuine, but she was certain that it was mere craftiness—a craftiness that she had hitherto admired, but which now awakened a fierce anger in her heart.

"When was he shot?" he questioned quietly.

"Last night," she answered scornfully. "Of course that is a surprise to you too. An hour after you left he rode up to the cabin and fell from his horse at the edge of the porch. He had been shot twice—both times in the back." She laughed—almost hysterically. "Oh, you knew enough not to take chances with him in spite of your bragging—in spite of the reputation you have of being a 'two-gun' man!"

He winced under her words, his face whitening, his lips twitching, his hands clenched that he might not lose his composure. But in spite of the conflict that was going on within him at the moment he managed to keep his voice quiet and even. It was admirable acting, she thought, her eyes burning with passion—despicable, contemptible acting.

"I reckon I ain't the snake you think I am, ma'am," he said, looking steadily at her. "But I'm admittin' that mebbe you've got cause to think so. When I left Ben last night I shook hands with him, after fixin' up the difference we'd had. Why, ma'am," he went on earnestly, "I'd just got through tellin' him about you an' me figgerin' to get hooked up. An' do you think I'd shoot him after that? Why, if I'd been wantin' to shoot him I reckon there was nothin' to stop me while he was standin' there. He'd never knowed what struck him. I'm tellin' you that I didn't know he was shot; that—"

She made a gesture of impatience. "I don't think I care to hear any more," she said. "I heard the shots here on the porch. I suppose you were so far away at that time that you couldn't hear them?"

He writhed again under the scorn in her voice. But he spoke again, earnestly. "I did hear some shootin'," he said, "after I'd gone on a ways. But I reckoned it was Ben."

"What do you suppose he would be shooting at at that time of the night?" she demanded.

"Why, I don't remember that I was doin' a heap of wonderin' at that time about it," he returned hesitatingly. "Mebbe I thought he was shootin' at a sage-hen, or a prairie-dog—or somethin'. I've often took a shot at somethin' like that—when I've been alone that way." He took a step toward her, his whole lithe body alive and tingling with earnestness. "Why, ma'am, there's a big mistake somewheres. If I could talk to Ben I'm sure I could explain—"

She drew her skirts close and stepped back toward the door. "There is nothing to explain—now," she said coldly. "Ben is doing nicely, and when he has fully recovered you will have a chance to explain to him—if you are not afraid."

"Afraid?" he laughed grimly. "I expect, ma'am, that things look pretty bad for me. They always do when someone's tryin' to make 'em. I reckon there ain't any use of tryin' to straighten it out now—you won't listen. But I'm tellin' you this: When everything comes out you'll see that I didn't shoot your brother."

"Of course not," sneered the girl. "You did not shoot him. Stafford did not hire you to do it. You didn't come here, pretending that you had been bitten by a rattler, so that you might have a chance to worm yourself into my brother's favor—and then shoot him. You haven't been hanging around Bear Flat all summer, pretending to look for stray Two Diamond cattle. You haven't been trying to make a fool of me—" Her voice trembled and her lips quivered suspiciously.

"Well, now," said Ferguson, deeply moved; "I'm awful sorry you're lookin' at things like you are. But I wasn't thinkin' to try an' make a fool of you. Things that I said to you I meant. I wouldn't say things to a girl that I said to you if—"

She had suddenly stepped into the cabin and as suddenly reappeared holding the rifle that was kept always behind the door. She stood rigid on the porch, her eyes blazing through the moisture in them.

"You go now!" she commanded hotly; "I've heard enough of your lies! Get away from this cabin! If I ever see you around here again I won't wait for Ben to shoot you!"

Ferguson hesitated, a deep red mounting over the scarf at his throat. Then his voice rose, tingling with regret. "There ain't any use of me sayin' anything now, ma'am," he said. "You wouldn't listen. I'm goin' away, of course, because you want me to. You didn't need to get that gun if you wanted to hurt me—what you've said would have been enough." He bowed to her, not even looking at the rifle. "I'm goin' now," he concluded. "But I'm comin' back. You'll know then whether I'm the sneak you've said I was."

He bowed again over the pony's mane and urged the animal around the corner of the cabin, striking the trail that led through the flat toward the Two Diamond ranchhouse.

CHAPTER XXI

THE PROMISE

Ferguson heard loud talking and laughter in the bunkhouse when he passed there an hour after his departure from the Radford cabin in Bear Flat. It was near sundown and the boys were eating supper. Ferguson smiled grimly as he rode his pony to the corral gate, dismounted, pulled off the bridle and saddle, and turned the animal into the corral. The presence of the boys at the bunkhouse meant that the wagon outfit had come in—meant that Leviatt would have to come in—if he had not already done so.

The stray-man's movements were very deliberate; there was an absence of superfluous energy that told of intensity of thought and singleness of purpose. He shouldered the saddle with a single movement, walked with it to the lean-to, threw it upon its accustomed peg, hung the bridle from the pommel, and then turned and for a brief time listened to the talk and laughter that issued from the open door and windows of the bunkhouse. With a sweep of his hands he drew his two guns from their holsters, rolled the cylinders and examined them minutely. Then he replaced the guns, hitched at his cartridge belt, and stepped out of the door of the lean-to.

In spite of his promise to Mary Radford to the effect that he would return to prove to her that he was not the man who had attempted to kill her brother he had no hope of discovering the guilty man. His suspicions, of course, centered upon Leviatt, but he knew that under the circumstances

Mary Radford would have to be given convincing proof. The attempted murder of her brother, following the disclosure that he had been hired by Stafford to do the deed, must have seemed to her sufficient evidence of his guilt. He did not blame her for feeling bitter toward him; she had done the only thing natural under the circumstances. He had been very close to the garden of happiness—just close enough to scent its promise of fulfilled joy, when the gates had been violently closed in his face, to leave him standing without, contemplating the ragged path over which he must return to the old life.

He knew that Leviatt had been the instrument that had caused the gates to close; he knew that it had been he who had dropped the word that had caused the finger of accusation to point to him. "Stafford didn't hire you to do it," Mary Radford had said, ironically. The words rang in his ears still. Who had told her that Stafford had hired him to shoot Radford? Surely not Stafford. He himself had not hinted at the reason of his presence at the Two Diamond. And there was only one other man who knew. That man was Leviatt. As he stood beside the door of the lean-to the rage in his heart against the range boss grew more bitter, and the hues around his mouth straightened more grimly.

A few minutes later he stalked into the bunkhouse, among the men who, after finishing their meal, were lounging about, their small talk filling the room. The talk died away as he entered, the men adroitly gave him room, for there was something in the expression of his eyes, in the steely, boring glances that he cast about him, that told these men, inured to danger though they were, that the stray-man was in no gentle mood. He dropped a short word to the one among them that he knew best, at which they all straightened, for through the word they knew that he was looking for Leviatt.

But they knew nothing of Leviatt beyond the fact that he and Tucson had not accompanied the wagon to the home ranch. They inferred that the range boss and Tucson had gone about some business connected with the cattle. Therefore Ferguson did not stop long in the bunkhouse.

Without a word he was gone, striding rapidly toward the ranchhouse. They looked after him, saying nothing, but aware that his quest for Leviatt was not without significance.

Five minutes later he was in Stafford's office. The latter had been worrying about him. When Ferguson entered the manager's manner was a trifle anxious.

"You seen anything of Radford yet?" he inquired.

"I ain't got anything on Radford," was the short reply.

His tone angered the manager. "I ain't askin' if you've got anything on him," he returned. "But we missed more cattle yesterday, an' it looks mighty suspicious. Since we had that talk about Radford, when you told me it wasn't him doin' the rustlin' I've changed my mind a heap. I'm thinkin' he rustled them cattle last night."

Ferguson looked quizzically at him. "How many cattle you missin'?" he questioned.

Stafford banged a fist heavily down upon his desk top. "We're twenty calves short on the tally," he declared, "an' half a dozen cows. We ain't got to the steers yet, but I'm expectin' to find them short too."

Ferguson drew a deep breath. The number of cattle missing tallied exactly with the number he had seen in the basin down the river. A glint of triumph lighted his eyes, but he looked down upon Stafford, drawling:

"You been doin' the tallyin'?"

"Yes."

Ferguson was now smiling grimly.

"Where's your range boss?" he questioned.

"The boys say he rode over to the river lookin' for strays. Sent word that he'd be in to-morrow. But I don't see what he's got to do—"

"No," returned Ferguson, "of course. You say them cattle was rustled last night?"

"Yes." Stafford banged his fist down with a positiveness that left no doubt of his knowledge.

"Well, now," observed Ferguson, "an' so you're certain Radford rustled them." He smiled again saturninely.

"I ain't sayin' for certain," returned Stafford, puzzled by Ferguson's manner. "What I'm gettin' at is that there ain't no one around here that'd rustle them except Radford."

"There ain't no other nester around here that you know of?" questioned Ferguson.

"No. Radford's the only one."

Ferguson lingered a moment. Then he walked slowly to the door. "I reckon that's all," he said. "To-morrow I'm goin' to show you your rustler."

He had stepped out of the door and was gone into the gathering dusk before Stafford could ask the question that was on the end of his tongue.

CHAPTER XXII

KEEPING A PROMISE

Ferguson's dreams had been troubled. Long before dawn he was awake and outside the bunkhouse, splashing water over his face from the tin wash basin that stood on the bench just outside the door. Before breakfast he had saddled and bridled Mustard, and directly after the meal he was in the saddle, riding slowly toward the river.

Before very long he was riding through Bear Flat, and after a time he came to the hill where only two short days before he had reveled in the supreme happiness that had followed months of hope and doubt. It did not seem as though it had been only two days. It seemed that time was playing him a trick. Yet he knew that to-day was like yesterday—each day like its predecessor—that if the hours dragged it was because in the bitterness of his soul he realized that today could not be—for him—like the day before yesterday; and that succeeding days gave no promise of restoring to him the happiness that he had lost.

He saw the sun rising above the rim of hills that surrounded the flat; he climbed to the rock upon which he had sat—with her—watching the shadows retreat to the mountains, watching the sun stream down into the clearing and upon the Radford cabin. But there was no longer beauty in the picture—for him. Hereafter he would return to that life that he had led of old; the old hard life that he had known before his brief romance had given him a fleeting glimpse of what might have been.

Many times, when his hopes had been high, he had felt a chilling fear that he would never be able to reach the pinnacle of promise; that in the end fate would place before him a barrier—the barrier in the shape of his contract with Stafford, that he had regretted many times.

Mary Radford would never believe his protest that he had not been hired to kill her brother. Fate, in the shape of Leviatt, had forestalled him there. Many times, when she had questioned him regarding the hero in her story, he had been on the point of taking her into his confidence as to the reason of his presence at the Two Diamond, but he had always put it off, hoping that things would be righted in the end and that he would be able to prove to her the honesty of his intentions.

But now that time was past. Whatever happened now she would believe him the creature that she despised—that all men despised; the man who strikes in the dark.

This, then, was to be the end. He could not say that he had been entirely blameless. He should have told her. But it was not the end that he was now contemplating. There could be no end until there had been an accounting between him and Leviatt. Perhaps the men who had shot Ben Radford in the back would never be known. He had his suspicions, but they availed nothing. In the light of present circumstances Miss Radford would never hold him guiltless.

Until near noon he sat on the rock on the crest of the hill, the lines of his face growing more grim, his anger slowly giving way to the satisfying calmness that comes when the mind has reached a conclusion. There would be a final scene with Leviatt, and then—

He rose from the rock, made his way deliberately down the hillside, mounted his pony, and struck the trail leading to the Two Diamond ranchhouse.

About noon Leviatt and Tucson rode in to the Two Diamond corral gate, dismounted from their ponies, and proceeded to the bunkhouse for dinner. The men of the outfit were already at the table, and after washing their faces from the tin wash basin on the bench outside the door, Leviatt and Tucson entered the bunkhouse and took their places. Greetings were given and returned through the medium of short nods—with several of the men even this was omitted. Leviatt was not a popular range boss, and there were some of the men who had whispered their suspicions that the death of Rope Jones had not been brought about in the regular way. Many of them remembered the incident that had occurred between Rope, the range boss, Tucson, and the new stray-man, and though opinions differed, there were some who held that the death of Rope might have resulted from the ill-feeling engendered by the incident. But in the absence of proof there was nothing to be done. So those men who held suspicions wisely refrained from talking in public.

Before the meal was finished the blacksmith poked his head in through the open doorway, calling: "Ol' Man wants to see Leviatt up in the office!"

The blacksmith's head was withdrawn before Leviatt, who had heard the voice but had not seen the speaker, could raise his voice in reply. He did not hasten, however, and remained at the table with Tucson for five minutes after the other men had left. Then, with a final word to Tucson, he rose and strode carelessly to the door of Stafford's office. The latter had been waiting with some impatience, and at the appearance of the range boss he shoved his chair back from his desk and arose.

"Just come in?" he questioned.

"Just come in," repeated Leviatt drawling. "Plum starved. Had to eat before I came down here."

He entered and dropped lazily into a chair near the desk, stretching his legs comfortably. He had observed in Stafford's manner certain signs of a subdued excitement, and while he affected not to notice this, there was a glint of feline humor in his eyes.

"Somebody said you wanted me," he said. "Anything doin'?"

Stafford had held in as long as he could. Now he exploded.

"What in hell do you suppose I sent for you for?" he demanded, as, walking to and fro in the room, he paused and glared down at the range boss. "Where you been? We're twenty calves an' a dozen cows short on the tally!"

Leviatt looked up, his eyes suddenly flashing. "Whew!" he exclaimed. "They're hittin' them pretty heavy lately. When was they missed?"

Stafford spluttered impotently. "Night before last," he flared. "An' not a damned sign of where they went!"

Leviatt grinned coldly. "Them rustlers is gettin' to be pretty slick, ain't they?" he drawled.

Stafford's face swelled with a rage that threatened to bring on apoplexy. He brought a tense fist heavily down upon his desk top.

"Slick!" he sneered. "I don't reckon they're any slick. It's that I've got a no good outfit. There ain't a man in the bunch could see a rustler if he'd hobbled a cow and was runnin' her calf off before their eyes!" He hesitated to gain breath before continuing. "What have I got an outfit for? What have I got a range boss for? What have I got—!"

Leviatt grinned wickedly and Stafford hesitated, his hand upraised.

"Your stray-man doin' anything these days?" questioned Leviatt significantly. "Because if he is," resumed Leviatt, before the manager could reply, "he ought to manage to be around where them thieves are workin'."

Stafford stiffened. He had developed a liking for the stray-man and he caught a note of venom in Leviatt's voice.

"I reckon the stray-man knows what he's doin'," he replied. He returned to his chair beside the desk and sat in it, facing Leviatt, and speaking with heavy sarcasm. "The stray-man's the only one of the whole bunch that's doin' anything," he said.

"Sure," sneered Leviatt; "he's gettin' paid for sparkin' Mary Radford."

"Mebbe he is," returned Stafford. "I don't know as I'd blame him any for that. But he's been doin' somethin' else now an' then, too."

"Findin' the man that's been rustlin' your stock, for instance," mocked Leviatt.

Stafford leaned back in his chair, frowning.

"Look here, Leviatt," he said steadily. "I might have spoke a little strong to you about them missin' cattle. But I reckon you're partly to blame. If you'd been minded to help Ferguson a little, instead of actin' like a fool because you've thought he's took a shine to Mary Radford, we might have been further along with them rustlers. As it is, Ferguson's been playin' a lone hand. But he claims to have been doin' somethin'. He ain't been in the habit of blowin' his own horn, an' I reckon we can rely on what he says. I'm wantin' you to keep the boys together this afternoon, for we might need them to help Ferguson out. He's promised to ride in to-day an' show me the man who's been rustlin' my cattle."

Leviatt's lips slowly straightened. He sat more erect, and when he spoke the mockery had entirely gone from his voice and from his manner.

"He's goin' to do what?" he questioned coldly.

"Show me the man who's been rustlin' my cattle," repeated Stafford.

For a brief space neither man spoke—nor moved. Stafford's face wore the smile of a man who has just communicated some unexpected and astonishing news and was watching its effect with suppressed enjoyment. He knew that Leviatt felt bitter toward the stray-man and that the news that the latter might succeed in doing the thing that he had set out to do would not be received with any degree of pleasure by the range boss.

But watching closely, Stafford was forced to admit that Leviatt did not feel so strongly, or was cleverly repressing his emotions. There was no sign on the range boss's face that he had been hurt by the news. His face had grown slightly paler and there was a hard glitter in his narrowed eyes. But his voice was steady.

"Well, now," he said, "that ought to tickle you a heap."

"I won't be none disappointed," returned Stafford.

Leviatt looked sharply at him and crossed his arms over his chest.

"When was you talkin' to him?" he questioned.

"Yesterday."

Leviatt's lips moved slightly. "An' when did you say them cattle was rustled?" he asked.

"Night before last," returned Stafford.

Leviatt was silent for a brief time. Then he unfolded his arms and stood erect, his eyes boring into Stafford's.

"When you expectin' Ferguson?" he questioned.

"He didn't say just when he was comin' in," returned Stafford. "But I reckon we might expect him any time."

Leviatt strode to the door. Looking back over his shoulder, he smiled evilly. "I'm much obliged to you for tellin' me," he said. "We'll be ready for him."

A little over an hour after his departure from the hill, Ferguson rode up to the Two Diamond corral gate and dismounted.

Grouped around the door of the bunkhouse were several of the Two Diamond men; in a strip of shade from the blacksmith shop were others. Jocular words were hurled at him by some of the men as he drew the saddle from Mustard, for the stray-man's quietness and invariable thoughtfulness had won him a place in the affections of many of the men, and their jocular greetings were evidence of this.

He nodded shortly to them, but did not answer. And instead of lugging his saddle to its accustomed peg in the lean-to, he threw it over the corral fence and left it. Then, without another look toward the men, he turned and strode toward the manager's office.

The latter was seated at his desk and looked up at the stray-man's entrance. He opened his lips to speak, but closed them again, surprised at the stray-man's appearance.

During the months that Ferguson had worked at the Two Diamond, Stafford had not seen him as he looked at this moment. Never, during the many times the manager had seen him, had he been able to guess anything of the stray-man's emotions by looking at his face. Now, however, there had come a change. In the set, tightly drawn lips were the tell-tale signs of an utterable resolve. In the narrowed, steady eyes was a light that chilled

Stafford like a cold breeze in the heat of a summer's day. In the man's whole body was something that shocked the manager into silence.

He came into the room, standing near the door, his set lips moving a very little, "You heard anything from Leviatt yet?" he questioned.

"Why, yes," returned Stafford, hesitatingly; "he was here, talkin' to me. Ain't been gone more'n half an hour. I reckon he's somewhere around now."

"You talkin' to him, you say?" said the stray-man slowly. He smiled mirthlessly. "I reckon you told him about them missin' calves?"

"I sure did!" returned Stafford with much vehemence. He laughed harshly. "I told him more," he said; "I told him you was goin' to show me the man who'd rustled them."

Ferguson's lips wreathed into a grim smile. "So you told him?" he said. "I was expectin' you'd do that, if he got in before me. That's why I stopped in here. That was somethin' which I was wantin' him to know. I don't want it to be said that I didn't give him a chance."

Stafford rose from his chair, taking a step toward the stray-man.

"Why, what—?" he began. But a look at the stray-man's face silenced him.

"I've come over here to-day to show you that rustler I told you about yesterday. I'm goin' to look for him now. If he ain't sloped I reckon you'll see him pretty soon."

Leviatt stepped down from the door of the manager's office and strode slowly toward the bunkhouse. On the way he passed several of the men, but he paid no attention to them, his face wearing an evil expression, his eyes glittering venomously.

When he reached the bunkhouse he passed several more of the men without a word, going directly to a corner of the room where sat Tucson and conversing earnestly with his friend. A little later both he and Tucson rose and passed out of the bunkhouse, walking toward the blacksmith shop.

After a little they appeared, again joining the group outside the bunkhouse. It was while Leviatt and Tucson were in the blacksmith shop that Ferguson had come in. When they came out again the stray-man had disappeared into the manager's office.

Since the day when in the manager's office, Ferguson had walked across the floor to return to Leviatt the leather tobacco pouch that the latter had dropped in the depression on the ridge above the gully where the stray-man had discovered the dead Two Diamond cow and her calf, Leviatt had known that the stray-man suspected him of being leagued with the rustlers. But this knowledge had not disturbed him. He felt secure because of his position. Even the stray-man would have to have absolute, damning evidence before he could hope to be successful in proving a range boss guilty of cattle stealing.

Leviatt had been more concerned over the stray-man's apparent success in courting Mary Radford. His hatred—beginning with the shooting match in Dry Bottom—had been intensified by the discovery of Ferguson on the Radford porch in Bear Flat; by the incident at the bunkhouse, when Rope Jones had prevented Tucson from shooting the stray-man from behind, and by the discovery that the latter suspected him of complicity with the cattle thieves. But it had reached its highest point when Mary Radford spurned his love. After that he had realized that just so long as the stray-man lived and remained at the Two Diamond there would be no peace or security for him there.

Yet he had no thought of settling his differences with Ferguson as man to man. Twice had he been given startling proof of the stray-man's quickness with the six-shooter, and each time his own slowness had been crushingly impressed on his mind. He was not fool enough to think that he could beat the stray-man at that game.

But there were other ways. Rope Jones had discovered that—when it had been too late to profit. Rope had ridden into a carefully laid trap and, in spite of his reputation for quickness in drawing his weapon, had found that the old game of getting a man between two fires had proven efficacious.

And now Leviatt and Tucson were to attempt the scheme again. Since his interview with Stafford, Leviatt had become convinced that the time for action had come. Ferguson had left word with the manager that he was to show the latter the rustler, and by that token Leviatt knew that the stray-man had gathered evidence against him and was prepared to show him to the manager in his true light. He, in turn, had left a message with the manager for Ferguson. "We'll be ready for him," he had said.

He did not know whether Ferguson had received this message. It had been a subtle thought; the words had been merely involuntary. By "We" the manager had thought that he had meant the entire outfit was to be held ready to apprehend the rustler. Leviatt had meant only himself and Tucson.

And they were ready. Down in the blacksmith shop, while Ferguson had ridden in and stepped into the manager's office, had Leviatt and Tucson made their plan. When they had joined the group in front of the bunkhouse and had placed themselves in positions where thirty or forty feet of space yawned between them, they had been making the first preparatory movement. The next would come when Ferguson appeared, to carry out his intention of showing Stafford the rustler.

To none of the men of the outfit did Leviatt or Tucson reveal anything of the nervousness that affected them. They listened to the rough jest, they laughed when the others laughed, they dropped an occasional word of encouragement. They even laughed at jokes in which there was no visible point.

But they did not move from their places, nor did they neglect to keep a sharp, alert eye out for the stray-man's appearance. And when they saw him come out of the door of the office they neglected to joke or laugh, but stood silent, with the thirty or forty feet of space between them, their faces paling a little, their hearts laboring a little harder.

When Ferguson stepped out of the door of the office, Stafford followed. The stray-man had said enough to arouse the manager's suspicions, and there was something about the stray-man's movements which gave the impression that he contemplated something more than merely pointing out the thief. If warning of impending tragedy had ever shone in a man's eyes, Stafford was certain that it had shone in the stray-man's during the brief time that he had been in the office and when he had stepped down from the door.

Stafford had received no invitation to follow the stray-man, but impelled by the threat in the latter's eyes and by the hint of cold resolution that gave promise of imminent tragedy, he stepped down also, trailing the stray-man at a distance of twenty yards.

Ferguson did not hesitate once in his progress toward the bunkhouse, except to cast a rapid, searching glance toward a group of two or three men who lounged in the shade of the eaves of the building. Passing the blacksmith shop he continued toward the bunkhouse, walking with a steady stride, looking neither to the right or left.

Other men in the group, besides Leviatt and Tucson, had seen the stray-man coming, and as he came nearer, the talk died and a sudden silence fell. Ferguson came to a point within ten feet of the group of men, who were ranged along the wall of the bunkhouse. Stafford had come up rapidly, and he now stood near a corner of the bunkhouse in an attitude of intense attention.

He was in a position where he could see the stray-man's face, and he marveled at the sudden change that had come into it. The tragedy had gone, and though the hard lines were still around his mouth, the corners twitched a little, as though moved by a cold, feline humor. There was a hint of mockery in his eyes—a chilling mockery, much like that which the manager had seen in them months before when in Dry Bottom the stray-man had told Leviatt that he thought he was a "plum man."

But now Stafford stood breathless as he heard the stray-man's voice, directed at Leviatt. "I reckon you think you've been some busy lately," he drawled.

Meaningless words, as they appear here; meaningless to the group of men and to the Two Diamond manager; yet to Leviatt they were burdened with a dire significance. They told him that the stray-man was aware of his duplicity; they meant perhaps that the stray-man knew of his dealings with the cattle thieves whom he had visited yesterday in the hills near the river. Whatever Leviatt thought, there was significance enough in the words to bring a sneering smile to his face.

"Meanin'?" he questioned, his eyes glittering evilly.

Ferguson smiled, his eyes unwavering and narrowing a very little as they met those of his questioner. Deliberately, as though the occasion were one of unquestioned peace, he drew out some tobacco and several strips of rice paper. Selecting one of the strips of paper, he returned the others to a pocket and proceeded to roll a cigarette. His movements were very deliberate. Stafford watched him, fascinated by his coolness. In the tense silence no sound was heard except a subdued rattle of pans in the bunkhouse—telling that the cook and his assistant were at work.

The cigarette was made finally, and then the stray-man lighted it and looked again at Leviatt, ignoring his question, asking another himself. "You workin' down the creek yesterday?" he said.

"Up!" snapped Leviatt. The question had caught him off his guard or he would have evaded it. He had told the lie out of pure perverseness.

Ferguson took a long pull at his cigarette. "Well, now," he returned, "that's mighty peculiar. I'd have swore that I seen you an' Tucson ridin' down the river yesterday. Thought I saw you in a basin in the hills, talkin' to some men that I'd never seen before. I reckon I was mistaken, but I'd have swore that I'd seen you."

Leviatt's face was colorless. Standing with his profile to Tucson, he closed one eye furtively. This had been a signal that had previously been agreed upon. Tucson caught it and turned slightly, letting one hand fall to his right hip, immediately above the butt of his pistol.

"Hell!" sneered Leviatt, "you're seein' a heap of things since you've been runnin' with Mary Radford!"

Ferguson laughed mockingly. "Mebbe I have," he returned. "Ridin' with her sure makes a man open his eyes considerable."

Now he ignored Leviatt, speaking to Stafford. "When I was in here one day, talkin' to you," he said quietly, "you told me about you an' Leviatt goin' to Dry Bottom to hire a gunfighter. I reckon you told that right?"

"I sure did," returned Stafford.

Ferguson took another pull at his cigarette—blowing the smoke slowly skyward. And he drawled again, so that there was a distinct space between the words.

"I reckon you didn't go around advertisin' that?" he asked.

Stafford shook his head negatively. "There ain't anyone around here knowed anything about that but me an' you an' Leviatt," he returned.

Ferguson grinned coldly. "An' yet it's got out," he stated quietly. "I reckon if no one but us three knowed about it, one of us has been gassin'. I wouldn't think that you'd done any gassin'," he added, speaking to Stafford.

The latter slowly shook his head.

Ferguson continued, his eyes cold and alert. "An' I reckon that I ain't shot off about it—unless I've been dreamin'. Accordin' to that it must have been Leviatt who told Mary Radford that I'd been hired to kill her brother."

Leviatt sneered. "Suppose I did?" he returned, showing his teeth in a savage snarl. "What are you goin' to do about it?"

"Nothin' now," drawled Ferguson. "I'm glad to hear that you ain't denyin' it." He spoke to Stafford, without removing his gaze from the range boss.

"Yesterday," he stated calmly, "I was ridin' down the river. I found a basin among the hills. There was a cabin down there. Four men was talkin' in front of it. There was twenty calves an' a dozen cows in a corral. Two of the men was—"

Leviatt's right hand dropped suddenly to his holster. His pistol was half out. Tucson's hand was also wrapped around the butt of his pistol.

But before the muzzle of either man's gun had cleared its holster, there was a slight movement at the stray-man's sides and his two guns glinted in the white sunlight. There followed two reports, so rapidly that they blended. Smoke curled from the muzzles of the stray-man's pistols.

Tucson sighed, placed both hands to his chest, and pitched forward headlong, stretching his length in the sand. For an instant Leviatt stood rigid, his left arm swinging helplessly by his side, broken by the stray-man's bullet, an expression of surprise and fear in his eyes. Then with a sudden, savage motion he dragged again at his gun.

One of the stray-man's guns crashed again, sharply. Leviatt's weapon went off, its bullet throwing up sand in front of Ferguson. Leviatt's eyes closed, his knees doubled under him, and he pitched forward at Ferguson's feet. He was face down, his right arm outstretched, the pistol still in his hand. A thin, blue wreath of smoke rose lazily from its muzzle.

Ferguson bent over him, his weapons still in his hands. Leviatt's legs stretched slowly and then stiffened. In the strained silence that had followed the shooting Ferguson stood, looking gloomily down upon the quiet form of his fallen adversary.

"I reckon you won't lie no more about me," he said dully.

Without a glance in the direction of the group of silent men, he sheathed his weapons and strode toward the ranchhouse.

CHAPTER XXIII

AT THE EDGE OF THE COTTONWOOD

Ferguson strode into the manager's office and dropped heavily into a chair beside the desk. He was directly in front of the open door and looking up he could see the men down at the bunkhouse congregated around the bodies of Leviatt and Tucson.

The end that he had been expecting for the past two days had come—had come as he knew it must come. He had not been trapped as they had trapped Rope Jones. When he had stood before Leviatt in front of the bunkhouse, he had noted the positions of the two men; had seen that they had expected him to walk squarely into the net that they had prepared for him. His lips curled a little even now over the thought that the two men had held him so cheaply. Well, they had learned differently, when too late. It was the end of things for them, and for him the end of his hopes. When he had drawn his guns he had thought of merely wounding Leviatt, intending to allow the men of the outfit to apply to him the penalty that all convicted cattle thieves must suffer. But before that he had hoped to induce Leviatt to throw some light upon the attempted murder of Ben Radford.

However, Leviatt had spoiled all that when he had attempted to draw his weapon after he was wounded. He had given Ferguson no alternative. He had been forced to kill the only man who, he was convinced, could have given him any information about the shooting of Radford, and now, in spite of anything that he might say to the contrary, Mary Radford, and even Ben himself, would always believe him guilty. He could not stay at Two Diamond now. He must get out of the country, back to the old life at the Lazy J, where among his friends he might finally forget. But he doubted much. Did men ever forget women they had loved? Some perhaps did, but he was certain that nothing—not even time—could dim the picture that was now in his mind: the hill in the flat, the girl sitting upon the rock beside him, her eyes illuminated with a soft, tender light; her breeze-blown hair—which he had kissed; which the Sun-Gods had kissed as, coming down from the mountains, they had bathed the hill with the golden light of the evening. He had thought then that nothing could prevent him from enjoying the happiness which that afternoon seemed to have promised. He had watched the sun sinking behind the mountains, secure in the thought that the morrow would bring him added happiness. But now there could be no tomorrow—for him.

Fifteen minutes later Stafford entered the office to find his stray-man still seated in the chair, his head bowed in his hands. He did not look up as the manager entered, and the latter stepped over to him and laid a friendly hand on his shoulder.

"I'm thankin' you for what you've done for me," he said.

Ferguson rose, leaning one hand on the back of the chair upon which he had been sitting. The manager saw that deep lines had come into his face; that his eyes—always steady before—were restless and gleaming with an expression which seemed unfathomable. But he said nothing until the manager had seated himself beside the desk. Then he took a step and stood looking into Stafford's upturned face.

"I reckon I've done what I came here to do," he said grimly. "I'm takin' my time now."

Stafford's face showed a sudden disappointment.

"Shucks!" he returned, unable to keep the regret from his voice. "Ain't things suited you here?"

The stray-man grinned with straight lips. He could not let the manager know his secret. "Things have suited me mighty well," he declared. "I'm thankin' you for havin' made things pleasant for me while I've been here. But I've done what I contracted to do an' there ain't anything more to keep me here. If you'll give me my time I'll be goin'."

Stafford looked up at him with a sly, significant smile. "Why," he said, "Leviatt told me that you'd found somethin' real interestin' over on Bear Flat. Now, I shouldn't think you'd want to run away from her!"

The stray-man's lips whitened a little. "I don't think Mary Radford is worryin' about me," he said steadily.

"Well, now," returned Stafford, serious again; "then I reckon Leviatt had it wrong."

"I expect he had it wrong," answered the stray-man shortly.

But Stafford did not yield. He had determined to keep the stray-man at the Two Diamond and there were other arguments that he had not yet advanced which might cause him to stay. He looked up again, his face wearing a thoughtful expression.

"I reckon you remember our contract?" he questioned.

The stray-man nodded. "I was to find out who was stealin' your cattle," he said.

Stafford smiled slightly. "Correct!" he returned. "You've showed me two thieves. But a while ago I heard you say that there was two more. Our contract ain't fulfilled until you show me them too. You reckon?"

The stray-man drew a deep, resigned breath. "I expect that's right," he admitted. "But I've told you where you can find them. All you've got to do is to ride over there an' catch them."

Stafford's smile widened a little. "Sure," he returned, "that's all I've got to do. An' I'm goin' to do it. But I'm wantin' my range boss to take charge of the outfit that's goin' over to ketch them."

"Your range boss?" said Ferguson, a flash of interest in his eyes, "Why, your range boss ain't here any more."

Stafford leaned forward, speaking seriously. "I'm talkin' to my range boss right now!" he said significantly.

Ferguson started, and a tinge of slow color came into his face. He drew a deep breath and took a step forward. But suddenly he halted, his lips straightening again.

"I'm thankin' you," he said slowly. "But I'm leavin' the Two Diamond." He drew himself up, looking on the instant more his old indomitable self. "I'm carryin' out our contract though," he added. "If you're wantin' me to go after them other two men, I ain't backin' out. But you're takin' charge of the outfit. I ain't goin' to be your range boss."

An hour later ten of the Two Diamond men, accompanied by Stafford and the stray-man, loped their horses out on the plains toward the river. It was a grim company on a grim mission, and the men forbore to joke as they rode through the dust and sunshine of the afternoon. Ferguson rode slightly in advance, silent, rigid in the saddle, not even speaking to Stafford, who rode near him.

Half an hour after leaving the Two Diamond they rode along the crest of a ridge of hills above Bear Flat. They had been riding here only a few minutes when Stafford, who had been watching the stray-man, saw him start suddenly. The manager turned and followed the stray-man's gaze.

Standing on a porch in front of a cabin on the other side of the flat was a woman. She was watching them, her hands shading her eyes. Stafford saw the stray-man suddenly dig his spurs into his pony's flanks, saw a queer pallor come over his face. Five minutes later they had ridden down through a gully to the plains. Thereafter, even the hard riding Two Diamond boys found it difficult to keep near the stray-man.

Something over two hours later the Two Diamond outfit, headed by the stray-man, clattered down into a little basin, where Ferguson had seen the cabin two days before. As the Two Diamond men came to within a hundred feet of the cabin two men, who had been at work in a small corral, suddenly dropped their branding irons and bolted toward the cabin. But before they had time to reach the door the Two Diamond men had surrounded them, sitting grimly and silently in their saddles. Several of Stafford's men had drawn their weapons, but were now returning them to their holsters, for neither of the two men was armed. They stood within the grim circle, embarrassed, their heads bowed, their attitude revealing their shame at having been caught so easily. One of the men, a clear, steady-eyed fellow, laughed frankly.

"Well, we're plum easy, ain't we boys?" he said, looking around at the silent group. "Corraled us without lettin' off a gun. That's what I'd call rediculous. You're right welcome. But mebbe you wouldn't have had things so easy if we hadn't left our guns in the cabin. Eh, Bill?" he questioned, prodding the other man playfully in the ribs.

But the other man did not laugh. He stood before them, his embarrassment gone, his eyes shifting and fearful.

"Shut up, you damn fool!" he snarled.

But the clear-eyed man gave no attention to this outburst. "You're Two Diamond men, ain't you?" he asked, looking full at Ferguson.

The latter nodded, and the clear-eyed man continued. "Knowed you right off," he declared, with a laugh. "Leviatt pointed you out to me one day when you was ridin' out yonder." He jerked a thumb toward the distance. "Leviatt told me about you. Wanted to try an' plug you with his six, but decided you was too far away." He laughed self-accusingly. "If you'd been half an hour later, I reckon you wouldn't have proved your stock, but we loafed a heap, an' half of that bunch ain't got our brand."

"We didn't need to look at no brand," declared Stafford grimly.

The clear-eyed man started a little. Then he laughed. "Then you must have got Leviatt an' Tucson," he said. He turned to Ferguson. "If Leviatt has been got," he said, "it must have been you that got him. He told me he was runnin' in with you some day. I kept tellin' him to be careful."

Ferguson's eyelashes twitched a little. "Thank you for the compliment," he said.

"Aw, hell!" declared the man, sneering. "I wasn't mushin' none!"

Stafford had made a sign to the men and some of them dismounted and approached the two rustlers. The man who had profanely admonished the other to silence made some little resistance, but in the end he stood within the circle, his hands tied behind him. The clear-eyed man made no resistance, seeming to regard the affair in the light of a huge joke. Once, while the Two Diamond men worked at his hands, he told them to be careful not to hurt him.

"I'm goin' to be hurt enough, after a while," he added.

There was nothing more to be done. The proof of guilt was before the Two Diamond men, in the shape of several calves in the small corral that still bore the Two Diamond brand. Several of the cows were still adorned with the Two Diamond ear mark, and in addition to this was Ferguson's evidence. Therefore the men's ponies were caught up, saddled, and the two men forced to mount. Then the entire company rode out of the little gully through which the Two Diamond outfit had entered, riding toward the cottonwood that skirted the river—miles away.

A little while before sunset the cavalcade rode to the edge of the cottonwood. Stafford halted his pony and looked at Ferguson, but the stray-man had seen enough tragedy for one day and he shook his head, sitting gloomily in the saddle.

"I'm waitin' here," he said simply. "There'll be enough in there to do it without me."

The clear-eyed man looked at him with a grim smile.

"Why, hell!" he said. "You ain't goin' in?" his eyes lighted for an instant. "I reckon you're plum white!" he declared. "You ain't aimin' to see any free show."

"I'm sayin' so-long to you," returned Ferguson. "You're game." A flash of admiration lighted his eyes.

The clear-eyed man smiled enigmatically. "I'm stayin' game!" he declared grimly, without boast. "An' now I'm tellin' you somethin'. Yesterday Leviatt told me he'd shot Ben Radford. He said he'd lied to Ben about you an' that he'd shot him so's his sister would think you done it. You've been white, an' so I'm squarin' things for you. I'm wishin' you luck."

For an instant he sat in the saddle, watching a new color surge into the stray-man's face. Then his pony was led away, through a tangle of undergrowth at the edge of the cottonwood. When Ferguson looked again, the little company had ridden into the shadow, but Ferguson could make out the clear-eyed man, still erect in his saddle, still seeming to wear an air of unstudied nonchalance. For a moment longer Ferguson saw him, and then he was lost in the shadows.

CHAPTER XXIV

THE END OF THE STORY

Two weeks later Ferguson had occasion to pass through Bear Flat. Coming out of the flat near the cottonwood he met Ben Radford. The latter, his shoulder mending rapidly, grinned genially at the stray-man.

"I'm right sorry I made that mistake, Ferguson," he said; "but Leviatt sure did give you a bad reputation."

Ferguson smiled grimly. "He won't be sayin' bad things about anyone else," he said. And then his eyes softened. "But I'm some sorry for the cuss," he added.

"He had it comin'," returned Ben soberly. "An' I'd rather it was him than me." He looked up at Ferguson, his eyes narrowing quizzically. "You ain't been around here for a long time," he said. "For a man who's just been promoted to range boss you're unnaturally shy."

Ferguson smiled. "I ain't paradin' around showin' off," he returned. "Someone might take it into their head to bore me with a rifle bullet."

Radford's grin broadened. "I reckon you're wastin' valuable time," he declared. "For I happen to know that she wouldn't throw nothing worse'n a posy at you!"

"You don't say?" returned Ferguson seriously. "I reckon—"

He abruptly turned his pony down the trail that led to the cabin. As he rode up to the porch there was a sudden movement, a rustle, a gasp of astonishment, and Mary Radford stood in the doorway looking at him. For a moment there was a silence that might have meant many things.

Both were thinking rapidly over the events of their last meeting at this very spot. Then Ferguson moved uneasily in the saddle.

"You got that there rifle anywheres handy?" he asked, grinning at her.

Her eyes drooped; one foot nervously pushed out the hem of her skirts. Then she laughed, flushing crimson.

"It wasn't loaded anyway," she said.

The sunset was never more beautiful than to-day on the hill in Bear Flat. Mary Radford sat on the rock in her accustomed place and stretched out, full length beside her, was Ferguson. He was looking out over the flat, at the shadows of the evening that were advancing slowly toward the hill.

She turned toward him, her eyes full and luminous. "I am almost at the end of my story," she said smiling at him. "But," and her forehead wrinkled perplexedly, "I find the task of ending it more difficult than I had anticipated. It's a love scene," she added banteringly; "do you think you could help me?"

He looked up at her. "I reckon I could help you in a real love scene," he said, "but I ain't very good at pretendin'."

"But this is a real love scene," she replied stoutly; "I am writing it as it actually occurred to me. I have reached the moment when you—I mean the hero—has declared his love for me,—of course (with a blush) I mean the heroine, and she has accepted him. But they are facing a problem. In the story he has been a cowpuncher and of course has no permanent home. And of course the reader will expect me to tell how they lived after they had finally decided to make life's journey together. Perhaps you can tell me how the hero should go about it."

"Do you reckon that any reader is that inquisitive?" he questioned.

"Why of course."

He looked anxiously at her. "In that case," he said, "mebbe the reader would want to know what the heroine thought about it. Would she want to go back East to live—takin' her cowpuncher with her to show off to her Eastern friends?"

She laughed. "I thought you were not very good at pretending," she said, "and here you are trying to worm a declaration of my intentions out of me. You did not need to go about that so slyly," she told him, with an earnestness that left absolutely no doubt of her determination, "for I am going to stay right here. Why," she added, taking a deep breath, and a lingering glance at the rift in the mountains where the rose veil descended, "I love the West."

He looked at her, his eyes narrowing with sympathy. "I reckon it's a pretty good little old country," he said. He smiled broadly. "An' now I'm to tell you how to end your story," he said, "by givin' you the hero's plans for the future. I'm tellin' you that they ain't what you might call elaborate. But if your inquisitive reader must know about them, you might say that Stafford is givin' his hero—I'm meanin', of course, his range boss—a hundred dollars a month—bein' some tickled over what his range boss has done for him.

"An' that there range boss knows when he's got a good thing. He's goin' to send to Cimarron for a lot of stuff—fixin's an' things for the heroine,—an' he's goin' to make a proposition to Ben Radford to make his cabin a whole lot bigger. Then him an' the heroine is goin' to live right there—right where the hero meets the heroine the first time—when he come there after bein' bit by a rattler. An' then if any little heroes or heroines come they'd have—"

Her hand was suddenly over his mouth. "Why—why—" she protested, trying her best to look scornful—"do you imagine that I would think of putting such a thing as that into my book?"

He grinned guiltily. "I don't know anything about writin'," he said, properly humbled, "but I reckon it wouldn't be any of the reader's business."

THE END.

BIBLIOBAZAAR

The essential book market!

Did you know that you can get any of our titles in large print?

Did you know that we have an ever-growing collection of books in many languages?

Order online:
www.bibliobazaar.com

Find all of your favorite classic books!

Stay up to date with the latest government reports!

At BiblioBazaar, we aim to make knowledge more accessible by making thousands of titles available to you- *quickly and affordably.*

Contact us:
BiblioBazaar
PO Box 21206
Charleston, SC 29413

CPSIA information can be obtained at www.ICGtesting.com
Printed in the USA
BVOW021236290612

293957BV00003B/39/A